'Kylie, there's a sizzling attraction between us. Why are you pretending it doesn't exist?'

She sucked in a harsh breath and tugged against Seth's hand. 'Don't,' she said softly. 'Don't do this.'

'Do what?'

'Make me fall for you.'

The seriousness of her tone made him drop her arm and take a step back. 'Okay, that's fine. Neither one of us is looking for a long-term relationship. Does that mean we can't have any fun?'

Dear Reader

Welcome to **Cedar Bluff Hospital**, located in a small Wisconsin town overlooking the beautiful rocky shores of Lake Michigan. MARRYING THE PLAYBOY DOCTOR is the first book in my new mini-series, and I really hope you enjoy reading about Seth and Kylie as much as I enjoyed writing about them.

Working as an emergency department physician, Seth Taylor sees first-hand how life is too short. Anything can happen, at any time, so his plan is to live life to the fullest. He likes fast cars and playing the field with women. Settling down in a serious relationship isn't a part of his plan—until he meets paramedic and single mum Kylie Germaine, and her six-year-old son Ben.

Kylie has been burned by Ben's father, who refused to stick around to help raise their son, so learning to trust Seth isn't easy. But soon she's forced to accept Seth's help with Ben. Can Kylie convince Seth that life isn't worth living without love?

I hope you enjoy MARRYING THE PLAYBOY DOCTOR, and look for the next two books in my *Cedar Bluff Hospital* series, coming out in September and October.

Happy Reading!

Laura

MARRYING THE PLAYBOY DOCTOR

BY
LAURA IDING

First published in Great Britain 2009
Harlequin Mills & Boon
Eton House, 18-24 Par

© Laura Iding 2009

ISBN: 978 0 263 2094

Set in Times Roman 1
15-0809-45476

Harlequin Mills & Boon policy is to use papers that are natural, renewable and recyclable products and made from wood grown in sustainable forests. The logging and manufacturing process conform to the legal environmental regulations of the country of origin.

Printed and bound in Great Britain
by CPI Antony Rowe, Chippenham, Wiltshire

Laura Iding loved reading as a child, and when she ran out of books she readily made up her own, completing a little detective mini-series when she was twelve. But, despite her aspirations for being an author, her parents insisted she look into a 'real' career. So the summer after she turned thirteen she volunteered as a Candy Striper, and fell in love with nursing. Now, after twenty years of experience in trauma/critical care, she's thrilled to combine her career and her hobby into one—writing Medical™ Romances for Mills & Boon. Laura lives in the northern part of the United States, and spends all her spare time with her two teenage kids (help!)—a daughter and a son—and her husband. Enjoy!

Recent titles by the same author:

EMERGENCY: SINGLE DAD, MOTHER NEEDED
THE SURGEON'S SECRET BABY WISH
THE FIREFIGHTER AND THE SINGLE MUM
BABY: FOUND AT CHRISTMAS

I'd like to dedicate this book
to the Milwaukee area WisRWA group.
Thanks for all your kind support and encouragement!

CHAPTER ONE

LIFE was too short.

Dr. Seth Taylor grimly watched the patient being rolled into trauma bay number two. From the paramedic report, he saw the woman on the gurney was only fifty-seven—the same age his mother had been when she'd unexpectedly died six months ago.

Ignoring the knot in his stomach, he stepped forward to take charge of the resuscitation.

"Hold CPR. What's her underlying rhythm?"

"Still PEA," a honey-blond female paramedic said as she climbed off the gurney from her position doing CPR. PEA was the acronym for pulseless electrical activity, which basically meant the electrical system of the heart was working, but the heart wasn't actually pumping any blood.

"Get a set of labs, stat, continue CPR and give me a history." Seth scowled, hoping this wasn't another cerebral aneurysm like his mother had suffered. "We need to find the source of her PEA."

"Labs are in process," one of the nurses said. "Her

pulse ox is low at eighty-two percent, despite being on one hundred percent oxygen."

"Double-check the tube placement," Seth ordered. "Did she have surgery recently? Is there a reason she might have thrown a pulmonary embolus or a tension pneumothorax?"

"No surgery, according to the husband, and no other reason to have a blood clot or tension pneumo that we're aware of." The female paramedic responded without hesitation. "Her history is fairly benign. The only complaint she had prior to passing out was nausea, lasting from the night before, and some vague complaint about neck pain, so our working assumption was that she'd suffered a myocardial infarction."

Since women experiencing a heart attack generally didn't present with the same symptoms of crushing chest pain, shortness of breath and dizziness as most men did, Seth was forced to consider the paramedic might have nailed it right. The honey-blonde looked young, with her hair tied back in a bouncy ponytail, but she obviously knew her stuff. A myocardial infarction would explain the patient's lack of oxygenation.

"Should I get a cardiology consult?" asked Alyssa, the brunette trauma nurse beside him.

Cedar Bluff Hospital, located in the less populated rural area off the shores of Lake Michigan, only had two cardiologists on staff, and if their patient needed something complicated like open heart surgery they'd end up transporting her to Milwaukee.

"Yeah, tell them they need to get down here ASAP.

Make sure a troponin level and cardiac enzymes are being run on the blood sample, too."

Alyssa hurried off, and he continued running their resuscitation efforts. "Let's give a dose of epinephrine and get a chest X-ray. Have we verified tube placement?"

"I did when I placed the tube."

The female paramedic's tone was defensive. He didn't have time to tell her not to take it personally. He would have verified anyone's ET tube placement, even his own.

"I've listened. There are breath sounds bilaterally," Cynthia, another trauma nurse, spoke up.

Alyssa returned. "Dr. Hendricks is on the way."

He nodded, somewhat relieved his colleague and friend Michael Hendricks happened to be the cardiologist on call today. He trusted Michael's judgment and didn't mind the extra help.

A radiology tech wheeled in a portable X-ray machine. As they shot a quick chest X-ray, another nurse spoke up. "Lab results are back. Electrolytes are a little abnormal, her potassium is low, but her hemoglobin is within normal range so she's probably not bleeding."

Seth took a deep breath. Okay. So far they'd ruled out two of the six possible causes of PEA. "What about her troponin and cardiac enzymes?"

"They're still being processed."

He pinned the radiology tech with a fierce gaze. "I want to see that film *now*."

The young tech nodded and scurried off, downloading the image onto the designated radiology computer terminal. Seth waited, and was forced to admit technology was amazing when the chest film image was available on the screen in less than a minute.

"No tension pneumothorax. There might be some blood around the heart, though." Finally a potential diagnosis. Cardiac tamponade was a potential cause of PEA. He spun back toward the patient. "I'm going to do a pericardial tap, to see if that helps."

He drew on a pair of sterile gloves as the nurse on the right side of the patient pulled out a sterile cardiac needle and syringe, carefully opening the packages so he could grab the items. The nurse on the other side of the patient doused her chest with an antibiotic solution while he connected the needle and syringe and picked out his landmarks. He took a quick, steady breath and slid the needle into the V beneath her sternum, hoping and praying he didn't cause more harm than good. When he saw the flash of blood, though, he knew he'd hit the right spot. Pulling back on the syringe, he drew out a good fifty milliliters of blood.

"Nice job," Michael drawled from behind him. "Why did you bother calling me?"

Seth spared his friend a quick, exasperated glance before putting another syringe on the needle to see if there was more blood to be removed. He withdrew another eighteen cc and then glanced up at the heart monitor. "Hold off on CPR. Let's see if she finally has a blood pressure and pulse to go with her rhythm."

There was a moment of complete silence as several staff members, including Michael, felt for a return of the patient's pulse.

"I feel a pulse, but it's weak." Michael spoke up.

Alyssa nodded, confirming she felt it, too.

"She has a blood pressure, but it's only sixty-five systolic," Cynthia added.

"Start a dopamine drip, and find out what that troponin level is." Seth stepped back and stripped off his sterile gloves. "Michael, our working diagnosis so far is an acute myocardial infarction with a pericardial effusion. I called you so you can take her to the cath lab if needed."

"It would be nice to see the troponin first," Michael said.

"I have it—her troponin is 0.51, which has been reported as critical," Alyssa informed them.

The number didn't sound high, but anything over 0.03 was considered indicative of an MI, so 0.51 was way above the accepted range.

Seth glanced at his friend. Michael nodded, under-standing his unspoken question. "Okay, she's mine now. Let's prepare to get her transferred immediately to the cath lab."

The nurses sprang into action, placing the patient on a portable heart monitor and then gathering all their paper-work together. Seth noticed the female paramedic stood off to the side, watching as the events unfolded. Once the cardiology team had taken over Seth could sign off on the case, although he knew the odds weren't in this poor woman's favor. She wasn't out of the woods yet. It was a sad fact that women who suffered from acute myocardial infarctions had a much lower survival rate than men, mostly because of their atypical presenting symptoms. At least in this case the paramedics had realized the potential and had treated the patient accordingly.

"Excuse me? Dr. Seth Taylor?"

He turned when he realized the female paramedic was speaking to him. "Yes?"

She held out her hand. "I'm Kylie Germaine, the new paramedic education coordinator here in Cedar Bluff."

This was Kylie Germaine? He'd seen the honey-blonde a couple of times but he hadn't known her name. He'd heard about a new paramedic education coordinator coming on board, but for some reason he'd expected someone older, more experienced. Kylie looked too young to have the expertise needed to provide education and training for the entire paramedic team. But then again she had pegged this particular patient's diagnosis correctly.

"Nice to meet you." He took her hand in his, feeling a slight jolt at the brief contact. He let go and took a step back, wondering if she'd felt the brief sizzle, too. "Nice call on the MI—helped steer us in the right direction."

"Thanks." A small smile tugged the corner of her mouth. "I'll confess, my partner thought I was nuts."

He raised a brow. "I guess you proved him wrong, didn't you?" Her ringless fingers made him smile. He liked her. She might be young, but Kylie was gorgeous, and he hadn't gone out on a date in what seemed like forever. He was on the verge of asking if she'd like to get together for a drink when she continued speaking.

"As part of my job I have started setting up meetings with each of the ED physicians, to get insight into potential training needs. I believe you and I are scheduled to meet in a couple of hours?"

They were? Seth wasn't always very good at keeping

up with his calendar. "Uh—yeah. A couple of hours." He glanced at his watch and rubbed the back of his neck. "Actually, I'm free now, if you have time."

"Now?" Kylie didn't look happy at the abrupt change in plans.

"We could wait until later. But you need to know patient care comes first. If I'm needed in the trauma room then we'll have to reschedule anyway."

Cedar Bluff only had one hospital, and they provided the only level two trauma services within a seventy-five mile radius. They stayed busy—especially in the height of the tourist season.

Seth swept a pointed glance around the momentarily empty trauma bay. "Your choice."

She narrowed her gaze, but nodded. "Give me a minute to talk to my partner, then."

He could wait, and he watched as she went back to talk briefly to the short guy who'd brought the patient in with her. Actually, now that the resuscitation was over he couldn't even remember noticing the other paramedic at all, only Kylie. Perky ponytail and youthful face aside, Kylie had certainly taken the lead in the situation.

He was glad she'd stopped by to talk with him.

She returned a few minutes later. "Okay, I'm ready."

"Great." He tried to soften her up with a smile. "My office is just down the hall." He waved to a short hallway off to the right.

She preceded him down the hall, and he had a hard time pulling his gaze from her swinging ponytail. He found himself thinking how to best approach her—

because he was interested in getting to know young-miss-paramedic-liaison better.

And, as he knew only too well, life was too short not to go after what you wanted.

Kylie was far too conscious of Dr. Seth Taylor following behind her as she made her way to his office.

Maybe he *was* a good-looking guy, with his broad shoulders, dark brown wavy hair and deep brown eyes, but she wasn't interested. She'd just moved to the quiet rural town of Cedar Bluff from the crime-laden city of Chicago, and she didn't have time for men.

Of course if he knew she was the single mother of a six-year-old Kylie had no doubt Seth Taylor would back off in a hurry. Most men did. Which suited her just fine.

She found his office and walked in through the open door, taking a seat as he made his way around to the other side of his desk.

"So, Kylie." His smile lit up his whole face. "How can I help you?"

His smile was lethal, and she was shocked to feel the impact all the way down to her toes. She licked her lips and struggled to remember why she was here. Seth Taylor had the uncanny knack of making her feel like she was in high school again, garnering the attention of the quarterback of the football team.

Focus, Kylie. Focus. She cleared her throat. "One of my goals is to revamp our training program, and I guess I'd like your opinion on any deficiencies you might have noticed in the crew."

"Deficiencies, huh?" Seth drummed his fingers on

the desk. "One area we can all stand to review is how women suffering an acute MI present differently than men. Today was a prime example."

She nodded. "Yes, I've already made a note of that—considering how Jim thought I was crazy to think along those lines."

Truthfully, she hadn't been too impressed with Jim's performance today, and hoped he wasn't an indication of how all the paramedics in Cedar Bluff worked. If so, she was in for a long haul to bring their skills up to what she considered an acceptable level.

"What about intubation techniques? You questioned my placement of the ET tube."

"Kylie, don't take it personally," he chided gently. "Double-checking endotracheal tube placement is routine for any resuscitation, especially if the patient is experiencing persistent hypoxia. If you're asking me if I've seen many tubes placed incorrectly by the paramedics, I'd have to say no, I haven't."

"Then what *have* you seen?" she challenged. "There must be some areas for improvement you'd like to discuss."

"There are, actually, several areas of improvement needed." Seth leaned forward, shooting another of his dazzling smiles. "But I'll need some time to get my thoughts together. Maybe we can talk about this later—say, over dinner tonight?"

What? Her mouth dropped open. Was he actually *hitting* on her?

"I'm sorry, I'm not available this evening," she said coolly. As a professional, she didn't appreciate his assumption she'd be willing to drop everything to go out with him. What was it with some men? Ben's father had been charming, too, but look how *that* had turned out. Not good. "However, I'd be happy to reschedule this meeting to another time that's more convenient for you."

Seth stared at her for a long moment, and then flashed a cajoling smile. "I suppose lunch tomorrow is out of the question, too?"

She narrowed her gaze, not finding his self-deprecating humor the least bit amusing. Seth Taylor was handsome, and obviously, from what she'd seen in the trauma room, a very capable ED physician. But why ask her out? Did he see her as some sort of easy mark? Or was he like this with all women? "Dr. Taylor, I'm not interested in sharing a meal with you. All I want to know is what areas of improvement you see for education and training in our paramedic crew."

"Okay." He lifted his hand as if in surrender. "Let me think about this for a minute."

She was glad he dropped the flirtatious smile and sat back in his chair. He idly doodled on the slip of paper in front of him.

"One thing that I'd personally like to see is for the paramedic crew to start using hypothermia on all resuscitated patients."

"Hypothermia?" Kylie sat up straighter, her interest piqued in spite of her annoyance. "In what way?"

Seth lifted a shoulder. "There are devices that can be placed over a patient right in the field to start bringing their temperature down."

They'd been talking about instituting a hypothermia

protocol in Chicago when she'd left. How amazing to discover that even small-town Cedar Bluff was up on the latest resuscitation techniques. "I'd love to institute some sort of protocol. Do you have one already written up?"

"Not yet. But I'd be happy to work on one with you."

His smile wasn't entirely innocent, yet at the same time she couldn't let such a fantastic opportunity pass by. "I'd love to help create a protocol. Anything we can do in the field to save lives is worth the effort."

"I agree." Seth raised a brow. "I'm not trying to cross your boundaries—clearly you're already involved in a relationship—but my schedule is tight. We may need to meet over a lunch hour, since that might be the only available option."

Kylie stared at him suspiciously, wondering if he was really being sincere or if he was simply probing for more information. Either way, it didn't really matter. This job was a promotion for her, and since her sole reason for taking the job and moving to a safe, rural area was to provide a better home life for Ben, she wasn't about to do anything to mess it up.

Which included falling for Seth Taylor's not-so-subtle charm.

"I do have a man in my life," she said, playing along with his assumption. The man was her six-year-old son, but Seth didn't need to know that. "I'll try to be as flexible as possible, though, in order to meet your needs."

"Great. You're a beautiful woman, Kylie, and I'm sorry if I made you uncomfortable." Seth pulled out his PDA and scrolled the buttons on the tiny screen. "Okay, how does next Monday work for you? Say about twelve-thirty?"

Beautiful? He'd actually called her beautiful? No man, not even Ben's father, had ever used that word to describe her. Cute—pretty, maybe, in a girl-next-door type of way—but never beautiful.

Seth Taylor was charming, and she was just beginning to realize how dangerous his smooth charm really was—especially when she was feeling at her most vulnerable. Living in a new town, with people she didn't know, wasn't easy. And she'd been so focused on helping her son adjust to his new day care that she hadn't done anything for herself. Luckily she wasn't interested in relationships, or she might have been tempted.

She found her voice. "Monday at twelve-thirty is perfect. Thank you."

As she stood and moved to leave, he called out, "Kylie?"

She turned. "Yes?"

"I hope the man in your life realizes how lucky he is."

She doubted Ben would think so. At least not in the way Seth meant. But she nodded and quickly escaped before she blabbed the truth.

If Seth knew she didn't really have a man in her life outside her son, Ben, then he might just continue his charming assault on her defenses.

And she wasn't too certain she possessed the strength to withstand a second attack.

CHAPTER TWO

SETH finished the rest of his shift and then made his way to the cardiac cath labs located on the third floor, hoping he'd run into Michael. He wanted to know how their cardiac patient, Marilyn Warner, was doing.

His colleague, dressed in scrubs, walked out of the cath lab door as Seth came in. "Hey, Seth."

"Michael." Seth tucked his hands into the pockets of his lab coat as he turned to fall into step with Michael. "I've come to find out how Marilyn Warner is doing."

"You mean our patient from this morning?" When Seth nodded, Michael grimaced. "Not so good. She needed emergency surgery, so I had to send her off to Trinity Medical Center in Milwaukee via Air Flight."

Damn. Emergency surgery was not a good sign. Especially emergency open heart surgery, after a full arrest and resuscitation. Seth's shoulders slumped and he scrubbed a hand over his face. "I see. I don't suppose you've heard anything from the cardiothoracic team in Milwaukee yet?"

Michael shook his head. "No, but I've been busy. I just finished my last case for the day."

Seth understood. He'd been busy, too. The hospital census had been jumping lately, and the ED in particular had been one nonstop revolving door.

"Seth, she's not your mother," Michael said softly.

"I know." His sharp response caused Michael to raise his brows in surprise. Michael, along with many other hospital staff members, had attended the funeral. Seth had appreciated his colleague's support through the difficult time. "My mother didn't die of a heart attack. She had an aneurysm in her brain. But Marilyn is the same age, and I just wish we'd been quick enough to save her."

"You were." Michael clapped his hand on Seth's shoulder in a reassuring gesture. "We've given her a chance, Seth. Not just once, after you brought her back in the ED, but now again, in surgery. She could have died in the ambulance on the way over, or in the ED, or in the cath lab—but she didn't."

"Yeah." Yet with each setback her chances of survival grew slimmer. Seth knew his friend was right, but he couldn't get over the feeling that their efforts hadn't been good enough. Second-guessing yourself wasn't always helpful, though, so he tried to change the subject. "I hope you've been practicing your pitching. The big baseball game is only a week away."

Michael grinned. "As a matter of fact I have. Don't worry, we have a good chance of winning."

The Cedar Bluff Hospital's annual baseball game had become a highly competitive event. Each year the nurses challenged the physicians, and despite the gender differences—there were generally more women nurses than men, and more male physicians than female—the games were very close. The winning team got free meals in the hospital cafeteria for a month. Not that he really cared about the food, but Seth did like to win.

His motto was to live in the moment. Because life was too short for regrets.

"Do you want to head out to the batting cage?" Michael asked.

Seth glanced at his watch. "Not tonight. Maybe this weekend, though."

"You're on," Michael agreed. "See you later, then."

"Later," Seth echoed as he turned and strode toward the parking lot.

On the way home Seth's thoughts lingered on Kylie Germaine. He didn't like to be conceited, but it wasn't often he was shot down so completely at a first meeting. Women generally liked him. Too bad she was already in a relationship, because he hadn't felt that spark of attraction for anyone in a long time.

He drummed his fingers on the steering wheel as he headed for his condo, located just ten minutes from the hospital. He needed to forget about Kylie. There were always plenty of women to go out with. He'd never stayed with anyone for more than a few weeks anyway. There was a new nurse who'd started recently—what was her name? Cherry? Or Cheri? But even as he tried to picture the new nurse working up on the second floor he couldn't seem to dredge up his usual enthusiasm.

For some peculiar reason his libido seemed stuck on a particular honey-blonde who clearly wasn't interested.

* * *

Kylie woke up feeling a bit grumpy as she'd suffered a restless night's sleep—which was all Seth's fault, since his wicked smile had haunted her dreams.

Seth? *Seth?* What was wrong with her? What had happened to Dr. Taylor? She always addressed physicians by their formal title of Doctor—mostly because she felt that four years of premed, followed by four years of medical school, followed by even more years of residency and fellowship training meant they'd earned the title and deserved every bit of respect that went along with it.

So when had Dr. Taylor become Seth in her mind?

Muttering "Dr. Taylor" under her breath several times, in an effort to get his proper title embedded in her memory, she quickly showered and dressed.

Ben was eating a bowl of dry cereal when she dragged herself into the kitchen. "Don't you want some milk with that?" she asked.

Ben gave a good-natured shrug. "Okay."

She smiled and reached into the fridge. She was so lucky to have Ben. He was easygoing and happy to help himself to whatever food he wanted without being too picky about it.

"Am I going to day care today?" Ben wanted to know, once she'd doused his cornflakes with milk.

"No, I thought we'd stay home, since I have the day off."

For the summer, she'd enrolled Ben in a day care learning center, hoping he'd get to meet some of the other kids prior to school starting in just a few weeks.

But, thanks to the shift she'd picked up last Saturday, she had today—Thursday—off. Her plans were to spend a couple of hours researching hypothermia protocols, so that she would have something ready to show Seth—*Dr. Taylor*—when they met next week. She'd thought it would be nice to work from home for a change.

For a moment Ben almost looked disappointed about not going to day care, but when he finished his cereal he scampered into the living room to turn on cartoons.

She ate a small bowl of cereal, too, while waiting for the coffee to finish brewing. She poured herself a steaming mug before heading to the small office she'd set up in the third bedroom. With any luck she could discover what other hospitals and paramedic units had done before Ben tired of the Cartoon Network.

Thank heavens for cable.

Ben showed up in the doorway fifteen minutes later. "Mom, can I have some apple juice?"

She glanced up from her computer and nodded. "Yes. But don't forget the rule. All food and drinks stay in the kitchen."

Ben rolled his eyes and left. No more than five minutes later he was back. "Mom, the top of the pitcher is stuck. I can't get the apple juice out."

"I'll get it for you." She saved her work on the computer before heading into the kitchen. After prying up the stuck lid of the pitcher, she poured Ben's glass of juice and then returned to her office.

"Mom, can I go outside to swing on the swing set?" Ben asked a few minutes later.

She stifled a sigh. Ben was only six, and a short attention span came along with the territory. Besides, she could see the swing set in the front yard from her office window. She smiled at him. "Sure, but make sure you wear a jacket." Cedar Bluff was located close to the shores of Lake Michigan, and often the breeze off the lake was cooler than inland temperatures, even now in late summer. Knowing her son, he'd wear the jacket, but shed it the first chance he got.

She heard his footsteps go to the coat closet, and then heard the door slam behind him on his way outside. She breathed a little sigh of relief. Okay, now that Ben was outside maybe she could get this protocol started. When she heard the door slam again, a few minutes later, she braced herself.

"Mom, can I go over to Joey's house to play?"

She hesitated. "Is Joey's mom there to watch you?"

"I don't know, but I'll ask." Ben turned as if to rush out.

"Wait a minute, I'll come with you."

There was no sense in sitting there while Ben ran out and then back in again. She followed Ben outside. Joey Clairmont's house was the next house over to the right. She could see Joey riding his bike in the driveway, and also noted that Joey's older sister, Jenny, was sitting outside on the front porch, playing Barbies with another little girl.

Then she saw Missy Clairmont sitting outside in a lawn chair, chatting with someone on her cell phone. They'd met when Kylie had moved in last month, although she hadn't seen much of her chatty neighbor since starting her new job two weeks ago. Kylie waved at Missy, who acknowledged her with a smile and a wave back.

Satisfied that Missy was there to supervise the kids, she granted her permission. "Sure, Ben. Go ahead. You can play with Joey."

"Thanks, Mom." Ben ran over to Joey. The boy got off his bike and the two of them began talking, their heads close together, no doubt comparing notes on their latest trading cards.

She headed back to her office, feeling a little guilty over her plans to work. Maybe she should just scrap the whole idea of starting on the hypothermia protocol and spend the day with Ben instead?

Sighing, she rested her chin on her hand. Okay, the hypothermia protocol needed to be done—not to mention revamping the entire paramedic training program. She was being paid extra to have this level of responsibility, and that meant she needed to live up to her bosses' expectations. She'd give herself a couple hours to work on it this morning, and then make it up to Ben later. Maybe she could take Ben and Joey to the movies? There was a Disney film that had come out a week or so ago that Ben would love to see. Maybe they'd even splurge and ruin their dinner with a huge bucket of popcorn.

Feeling better, Kylie turned her attention back to the hypothermia protocol. She found several examples, and began printing them out to see what the similarities and differences were. She'd set up some meetings with the other ED physicians, too, and had received some good feedback.

Not one of *them* had even looked at her twice on a personal level—much less tried to hit on her the way Seth had.

Dr. Taylor. Get it through your head. He's Dr. Taylor!

She buried her persistent thoughts of Dr. Taylor and concentrated on her work. There were really only very minor differences in the two hypothermia protocols she'd gotten from other sources. Maybe this wouldn't take long to create at all.

A shrill scream split the air.

Ben? She sucked in a breath and sprang to her feet, running toward the living room. Through the picture window she saw a red bike crumpled beneath the back bumper of a car in the street outside Joey's house.

Dear God. A red bike. *Ben's* bike!

She tore outside, running straight to the scene of the accident. Her heart pounded in her chest and her vision went cloudy when she saw Ben's body sprawled on the asphalt, half under the car.

"Owwwww," he wailed.

"I'm sorry, lady, I didn't see him," the male driver of the car said, looking pale. "I called 911. They're sending an ambulance."

"Thanks. Shh, Ben. It's all right, I'm here." Kylie blinked, fighting to keep from losing control—especially when she saw the deep gash over Ben's left eye. Blood was everywhere, and she had to remind herself that head wounds always bled like crazy. Ben was also holding his left arm protectively across his chest. "I need some towels to put pressure on his head wound," she said to the group of onlookers who'd gathered around. She barely noticed when someone dashed off to the house, her attention focused on her son. "Don't move, honey. I need a minute to examine you."

She reached under the car, feeling his extremities. "Does your neck hurt? Or your back?" she asked.

"N-no. Just my—head and—my arm," Ben said between hiccupping sobs.

He was talking, and making sense, which went a long way to easing her panic. After ruling out a neck or back injury, she eased Ben from beneath the car, wincing at the copious amount of blood coating his face and soaking his shirt.

Missy Clairmont, Joey's mother, returned with an armload of towels, babbling about how she was so sorry, she hadn't realized the boys had taken their bikes out into the road, and she'd only run inside for a minute to use the bathroom. Kylie didn't respond except to nod at her, using one towel to hold pressure over Ben's eye and the other to mop up the worst of the blood.

Her hands were shaking.

In the distance she heard sirens, and knew help was on the way. She crushed Ben close, knowing she needed to check his pupils for signs of concussion but also needed to stem the bleeding from the cut over his eye, so he didn't lose too much blood. Rattled, she couldn't decide which threat was worse.

When the paramedics arrived, she was relieved they took control of the medical situation, leaving her to simply hold Ben in a comforting embrace. In mere minutes they had Ben bundled up and ready for transport.

No one argued when she climbed into the ambulance with him.

"His pupils are reactive, but the left one is larger

than the right," Randal, one of the older paramedics, said. "And I think he has a radial fracture in his left arm."

A concussion and a fracture didn't seem too bad, but Kylie knew that it was possible Ben's head injury could be worse than it looked. The only way to measure if he was bleeding into his brain was through a CT scan.

She clung to Ben's hand as they wound through the streets toward Cedar Bluff Hospital. She wondered if Seth was the physician on duty today.

She didn't know very many of the Cedar Bluff ED physicians yet, but she did know Seth. And she didn't want a stranger caring for her son.

Seth glanced at his pager to get the details of the most recent trauma call. *Six-year-old boy hit by a car. VSS. ETA two minutes.*

"Victoria, put this kid in the trauma room, okay?" he called to the nurse in charge.

She raised a brow. "His vitals are stable."

"I don't care. I want him in the trauma room." Seth would rather overreact than underestimate how sick a patient might be. Any child hit by a car had the potential to go bad in a hurry.

Seconds later Leila Ross, one of the general surgeons who'd cross-trained as a trauma surgeon, walked in. "Hear you have a peds patient on the way?"

"We do." Seth glanced at Leila, smiling at the petite surgeon who was lucky enough to be carrying the trauma pager for the day. "His vitals are stable, though."

"Good." Leila headed over to the sink to wash her hands and he watched for a moment, admiring her silky straight black hair, pulled back into a long braid. Leila was beautiful in an ethereal way, but as much as he'd enjoyed her company on the few dates they'd had, there hadn't really been a spark of attraction between them. Since they shared a mutual respect of each other's abilities, though, they'd decided they were better off remaining friends.

Besides, he'd often sensed Leila's dark troubled gaze held secrets she wasn't willing to share.

The doors to the trauma bay burst open and their newest arrival was wheeled in. It took him only two seconds to recognize Kylie, although she wasn't in her usual paramedic uniform. She wore a soft butter-yellow sweater smeared with blood and a pair of figure-hugging jeans.

"Six-year-old hit by a car while riding his bike. He has a laceration over his left eye and a minor concussion. His pupils are unequal but react to light." A tall male paramedic rattled off the detailed information. "He also has a possible fracture in his left arm."

Seth stepped forward to lift the blood-soaked towels to see the laceration, and winced when he saw the gap was large enough that he could see all the way into the child's orbital eye socket. "Back or neck pain?"

"Ben denies back or neck pain," Kylie said.

The paramedic glanced at her, and then added, "Ben has some minor scrapes on his left leg, but no other obvious signs of injury. The vehicle was backing up, so it wasn't going very fast."

He noticed the way Kylie clung to the boy's hand. "We'll need to get a stat CT of his head, and X-rays of his extremities, but I want to stitch up that head wound first."

Kylie paled at his words, but didn't let go as she met Seth's gaze. "I'm staying."

"Are you his mother?" he asked.

When she nodded, he didn't show his surprise, but took her arm to draw her away from the bedside. She reluctantly let go of Ben's hand.

"Is Ben's father on his way, too?" he asked, thinking that Kylie could use some support.

"No. His father left a long time ago." Her tone was matter-of-fact, with no sign of bitterness.

"Is there someone else I can call for you?" he persisted. "A friend? Anyone to be here so you don't have to go through this alone?"

"No, there isn't anyone to call. We just moved here a few weeks ago." She was barely paying attention to him, her gaze going back to her son. "I'm fine," she insisted, tugging to free herself from his grip. "But I'd really like to be there while you stitch him up."

Sometimes parents didn't do well when they stayed to watch, but knowing Kylie's paramedic background he quickly relented. "All right," he agreed, releasing her arm.

Kylie didn't hesitate, but went straight back to Ben's bedside, taking his hand and leaning down to press a soft kiss on her son's forehead.

Seth knew Kylie was distraught. She hadn't caught her slip-up, but he had.

She didn't have a man in her life.

But she did have a son.

Seth let out a sigh. He loved women, and loved having fun, but a family—especially a single mother with a young son—wasn't a part of his future.

He strode to Ben's bedside, calling for the facial suture tray, realizing Kylie was very much off-limits.

At least for him.

CHAPTER THREE

WATCHING Seth suture the laceration in Ben's eyebrow was the hardest thing she'd ever had to do.

But she hadn't made a fool of herself by passing out, although she'd definitely felt woozy for a few bad moments. Which was odd, since she'd seen her fair share of blood while on duty. No wonder they always asked family members to leave for these types of procedures. She'd felt every one of those five tiny stitches Seth had placed more than Ben had, since he'd been given lidocaine to numb the area.

Fighting nausea, she took a deep breath and let it out slowly. Seth had deemed Ben stable enough to be moved out of the trauma bay, and after the CT scan of his head they'd ended up in a small private room in the ED area. It felt strange to be sitting at his bedside, watching the activity all around, instead of being the one bringing patients in.

Now they were simply waiting for the CT scan results, and for the orthopedic surgeon to cast Ben's left arm. The break was actually fairly minor, not complex at all, but Ben would need to wear a cast for the next four to six weeks.

She closed her eyes and tried not to succumb to the overwhelming wave of guilt. Ben was okay. He wasn't hurt badly. He knew the rules—knew he shouldn't have been riding his bike on the road. She didn't blame Missy Clairmont, because the real fault was hers. If she hadn't been trying to impress Seth with having a hypothermia protocol finished in record time maybe she would have stayed outside to watch the boys herself, instead of depending on Joey's mother to do it.

"Kylie?" Seth called from the doorway.

She lifted her head and struggled to smile. "Hi. Do you have the CT results yet?"

He shook his head. "No, but I would like to put the cast on Ben's arm, if you don't object. The orthopedic surgeon is pretty far behind. He's telling me it'll be another couple of hours before he can break away to come down here."

Hours? Good grief—she and Ben had already been here for two and a half hours. At this rate it was amazing Cedar Bluff *ever* got patients out of the ED.

"I don't mind." The break was simple, and she didn't doubt that Seth wouldn't have offered to place the cast if he didn't know what he was doing. He might have an ego where women were concerned, but so far, from what she'd seen, his medical skills were solid.

"Great, I'll be right back." When he returned, he was pushing a bulky cart into Ben's room. "Hey, Ben. How are you feeling?"

Her son glanced over at Seth with his good eye. His

left eye was swollen and partially covered by the dressing over his incision. "Better," Ben answered, although his voice was a little slurred.

She sent Seth a wry look. "They gave him something for the pain and he's been a little loopy."

Seth grinned. "Hey, there's nothing wrong with being a little loopy." He turned his attention back to Ben. "So, Ben, tell me your favorite color. You get to pick what you want for your cast. Or—" he paused dramatically "—we can put this special Green Bay Packers gauze on. What do you think? Pretty cool, huh?"

Ben's brow puckered as he solemnly surveyed the options on the cast cart. "Doncha have Chicago Bears gauze?"

"Chicago Bears? *What?* You're kidding me, right? Chicago Bears?" Seth clasped his chest dramatically, staggering back a few steps as he stared at Ben in mock horror. "This is Wisconsin, son. What are you *thinking*? The Chicago Bears are the archenemy."

Ben giggled, as Seth had meant him to. "I *like* the Chicago Bears."

"You do realize Green Bay is only seventy-five miles north of here, don't you? Heck, the stadium is practically in our backyard."

Ben shrugged. Kylie doubted her son even understood how far seventy-five miles was. "I don't care."

"A Bears fan living in Cedar Bluff." Seth shook his head from side to side, pretending to be upset. "What is the world coming to? Sorry, Ben, we don't have any Chicago Bears gauze. But we do have navy blue and we do have orange."

"Yeah?" Ben's eyes lit up. "Blue and orange, the Bears colors. *That's* what I want on my cast."

"Okay." Seth let out a dramatic sigh. "But you're lucky I like you, Ben, because it's not going to be easy for me to help out a Chicago Bears fan." Seth went to work, setting the blue and orange gauze off to the side before slipping the stocking over Ben's small arm. "You have to promise not to tell anyone I did this for you, all right?"

Ben giggled again, and nodded earnestly. Watching Seth interact with her son made Kylie realize how much Ben missed having a father figure around. She hated to admit it, but she hadn't even known Ben *had* a favorite football team. It must be something they talked about at day care, because it wasn't as if she watched sports on TV on a regular basis.

Seth kept up a running commentary as he made the cast on Ben's arm. She could only watch helplessly as Ben reveled in Seth's male attention. Since his father had left before he was born, Ben didn't have *any* male role models in his life.

Guilt returned full force. Along with an edgy wariness. She didn't have a good track record as far as her choices in men went. She and Ben's father had dated for over a year, and had actually been just starting to talk about the future when she'd discovered she was pregnant. Tristan had completely changed during her pregnancy—seemingly overnight. Once charming and sweet, he turned sullen and resentful. When Tristan had finally left she'd felt lost, and alone, but also somewhat relieved. She'd thought he might change his mind once the baby was born, but he hadn't.

So she'd borne the stigma of having a child out of wedlock with her chin held high, refusing to think of Ben as a mistake.

Her son was the highlight of her life. The best thing to ever happen to her. He could *never* be a mistake.

And she didn't need a man in her life to be happy.

Seth finished the cast, telling Ben how he could use a permanent marker to write on the outside if he wanted, then joking that if he wanted to write the word "Bears" he'd have to ask for his mother's help, because he wasn't sure how to spell it and might accidentally write "Packers" instead. Then he rolled the cast cart back out of the room, promising to return soon.

Ben's eyelids drifted closed, so Kylie took advantage of the moment to rest her head on his bed, still holding on to his non-casted hand. Now that the adrenaline rush had faded, she felt as if she'd gone ten rounds in the ring with a boxer and lost every one.

She must have dozed a bit, because suddenly she felt a warm hand on her shoulder. "Wake up, Kylie."

Prying her eyes open, she blinked, focusing on Seth's face. His kindness was like a balm to her wounded soul. "I'm awake. Sorry. Do you have the results?"

He nodded and gave a reassuring smile. "Yes, and you'll be glad to know Ben's CT is clear. He's suffered a minor concussion, but there isn't any sign of a bleed."

"Thank heavens," she whispered. Glancing at her son, she noticed Ben was still asleep. The pain meds were no doubt making him drowsy.

"I'd still like Ben to see an ophthalmologist." Seth

frowned, his expression turning serious. "The cut over his eye is very deep, and once the swelling goes down he should see a specialist to make sure there isn't any damage to the eye—particularly the retina."

"All right." She stared at her son for a moment, before lifting her gaze to Seth's. "Thank you for everything. You did a wonderful job with him."

He smiled gently. "No problem. That's what I'm here for. Besides, he's a great kid."

"Yes, he is. When I saw his bike mangled beneath that car…" She swallowed hard and shook her head. "I was so scared."

"I can only imagine how awful that must have been."

His hand tightened on her shoulder for a moment, and she had the insane urge to rest her cheek against his arm, drawing from his seemingly endless strength.

"I'll get a nurse in here to go through the discharge paperwork."

Seth's hand dropped from her shoulder and she immediately felt the loss of his touch. "Take care of yourself, and follow up with Ben's pediatrician in a week."

"I will." She watched Seth leave, noting how serious he'd been since they'd arrived. There was no sign of the flirty charm he'd displayed with they'd first met.

Which was exactly what she wanted—for him to treat her as an equal. As a professional.

There was no reason to feel this sense of desolation at the change in Seth's demeanor.

It struck him, as Seth watched Kylie prepare to leave, packing up the supplies they'd given her for Ben's dressing changes, that since she'd come in on the ambulance with Ben she probably needed a ride home.

Cedar Bluff was a fairly small town. They didn't have a regular or reliable cab service. People always tended to help each other out when needed.

He glanced at the clock, thinking that he hadn't taken a lunch break yet. If Simon Carter, one of the other ED physicians, would cover for him, *he* could drive Kylie home.

He walked into the room while Kylie was asking a nurse about local bus routes.

"I'll drive you home," he said. "It's well past time for my lunch break anyway."

She hesitated, but then glanced at Ben, and he could practically see her weighing the options before she nodded. "If you don't mind, that would be great."

"I don't mind." He gathered up the bright Cedar Bluff Hospital bag stuffed with dressings, leaving her to carry Ben. "I'm in the employee lot, though, so why don't you wait here for a minute? I'll swing past the front doors to pick you up."

Somewhat dazed, she nodded, and he hustled off. A few minutes later he pulled up at the front door, hurrying out to give her a hand.

"You drive a cherry-red Corvette with a white leather interior?" she asked, half in awe, half exasperated. "Are you crazy? We can't ride in that. What if Ben gets sick or something?"

He hadn't even realized his car might not be suitable. "It doesn't matter. But you'll have to hold him on your lap, since Charlene doesn't have a backseat." Seth was used to disparaging comments about his penchant for fast cars, but he figured it was better than going bungee jumping or skydiving, like he'd been tempted to do for his twenty-eighth birthday last year. He intended to live life to the fullest, no matter what.

"It's illegal," she protested, hanging back. "And I'm worried. What if something happens to Ben?"

He mentally kicked himself for not thinking ahead about how Kylie might feel. Especially so soon after Ben's accident. "Do you want me to borrow a car?" He knew Leila drove a sedan.

"No, that's all right," she said slowly. "I guess we don't have a booster seat for him anyway. I'm sure we'll be fine."

He hesitated, but when she climbed in he simply closed the door behind her. He hurried around and slid into the driver's seat. "Don't worry. We'll be home before you know it."

"Okay, but don't speed." She clutched Ben tighter.

"I promise we'll go slow."

"I doubt your slow is the same as my slow," she muttered. "And I can't believe you named your car Charlene."

Seth flashed an unrepentant grin. "Why not? I name all my cars."

She rolled her eyes. "Figures. And I bet they're all female names, too."

"Of course." Did she really think a guy would name a car after another guy? Hello? No way, no how.

She shook her head, as if not understanding the male

psyche one bit. "I live off Ryerson and Birch, in a small subdivision off Highway 22."

He nodded, vaguely familiar with the area. She didn't say much as he drove, and before he knew it she was directing him to her house.

"Fourth on the north side of the street—the blue-gray ranch. I'm renting until I have enough for a down payment."

Smart not to overextend herself. He saw the mangled red bicycle off to the side of her driveway before he saw anything else. Geez, the kid had been lucky. If the car had been going faster, the boy's injuries would have been far more serious. He could only imagine how terrified Kylie must have been.

He could remember all too clearly the night the police had come to their house to tell them about the accident that had claimed his father's life. They'd all been teenagers, he the youngest of three. His older sister and older brother now lived in other parts of the country. His father's death had hit them all hard, but together they'd managed to weather the storm.

Kylie was alone, though. Who would have helped her if something awful had happened to her son?

No one. Losing the people you loved was difficult at any time, but he couldn't imagine anything worse than losing a child. All the more reason to keep his distance. Kylie and her son were a family, and he wasn't in the market for a family. He didn't know if he'd be a good father to his own kids, let alone someone else's son.

He'd offer friendship, nothing more.

"Do you need help?" he asked, when she awkwardly got out of the car.

"I can manage." She held Ben close, avoiding his gaze.

He went ahead, opening the front door for her, not surprised to find it unlocked. She would have been more concerned over Ben's welfare than about insignificant details.

"Thanks," she murmured, slipping past him to gently set Ben on the sofa.

He took a moment to glance around her cozy house, noticing one whole wall was dedicated to pictures of Kylie and Ben—mostly Ben.

None of the pictures included a father.

"Is there anything else you need?" He felt bad, just leaving her alone.

"Seth, I've raised Ben on my own for the past six years. Trust me, I'll be fine."

She'd raised Ben alone since he was born? The idea troubled him. Especially since she didn't seem to have a lot of money. Didn't the guy pay child support? Obviously not. He didn't really doubt Kylie was more than capable of raising Ben on her own, but it didn't make leaving any easier. "Don't forget to make that appointment for Ben to see an ophthalmologist."

"I won't." She walked him toward the door. "Thanks for the ride."

"You're welcome." He was oddly reluctant to leave. Where had his normally casual attitude toward women gone? He needed to get himself back on track, and quick. At the door he glanced back at her. "Kylie, since you're new to the area, feel free to give me a call if you need anything, okay?"

Her brow puckered in a puzzled frown. "Thanks, Seth. But, like I said, I'm sure we'll be fine."

He wanted to pull her into his arms for a reassuring hug, but they'd only just met the other day. He barely knew her. She was smart, and a good mother to Ben. Yet he knew she wasn't his type. She had responsibilities. He couldn't imagine Kylie going out and having a wild, fun night on the town.

But knowing that didn't change how he felt. He wanted to see her again. Outside of work.

He turned and left her house, walking quickly back to his car, knowing it was for the best not to take the seeds of their friendship any further.

No matter how tempted he was.

Kylie fed Ben a light dinner of tomato soup and half of a toasted cheese sandwich. Comfort food was always good when you were feeling sick. When he complained about his arm hurting she gave him some children's pain medicine.

All evening Ben talked nonstop about Dr. Seth. And football. She made a mental note to pay more attention to the football games on television, so she'd have a clue who the Packers and the Bears were. It was up to her to fulfill both parental roles in Ben's life.

Especially considering how easily Seth Taylor had made an impression on her young son.

Too bad Seth's entire attitude toward *her* had changed once he'd discovered she was a single mother. Her cheeks burned as she belatedly realized he now knew she'd lied to him about having a man in her life.

During the crisis with Ben she hadn't even thought twice about it when Seth had asked if there was someone he could call to be with her.

His gentle caring toward both her and Ben had been very sweet. Nice. Yet she imagined he was the same way with all his patients. She and Ben hadn't been anything special. Besides, he'd never even hinted that he was still interested in going out with her, the way he had when they'd first met.

The ache in her chest intensified. Ridiculous to feel hurt. Seth wasn't the first man to avoid her after finding out about Ben.

And she doubted he'd be the last.

Which was exactly what she wanted, right? Right.

Finally it was time to tuck Ben into bed. His eyes were practically sliding closed, yet he still talked about Dr. Seth.

"Mom? Do you think Dr. Seth would be willing to come over to play football with me and Joey?"

She reached over to smooth his hair away from the dressing covering the sutures above his left eye. "Have you forgotten your broken arm?" she asked dryly. "You won't be catching footballs for a while. Once your cast comes off *I'll* play with you."

"But you're a girl," Ben protested.

A difficult point to argue. And, really, what did she know about football? Not much. "What about Joey's dad? Doesn't he play football with you boys?"

"Sometimes. But Joey's dad goes on a lot of business trips. That's why I was hoping Dr. Seth would play with us." His earnestly hopeful face tugged at her heart.

"I don't know, Ben," she said, trying to let him down gently. "He's a very busy doctor at the hospital."

Ben scrunched up his face. "Doesn't he ever get a day off?"

"I'm sure he does. But you have to wait a few weeks for your cast to come off anyway, so let's not worry about that now. How about closing your eyes and getting some sleep? You'll need to go to day care tomorrow. I bet the kids will be excited to sign your cast."

Ben managed to smile, even as his heavy eyelids were already sliding closed. "G'night, Mom."

"Good night, Ben."

Two hours later she envied Ben's ability to sleep. She was still tossing and turning. Even a cup of her favorite tea didn't help. All she could think of was how much Ben must be missing having a father. Why else would he have become fixated on Seth so quickly?

She knew, better than her son, how much misplaced trust could hurt. Hadn't Tristan left her when she'd needed him the most? Seth was a nice guy, but that didn't mean he'd be a good choice to even consider starting a relationship with.

She needed to keep Seth at a safe distance.

For Ben's sake and her own.

CHAPTER FOUR

SETH had picked up an extra night shift for Simon Carter, who'd caught some sort of flu bug. He didn't mind giving up his Saturday—the ED staff possessed a strong culture of teamwork. The night had been steadily busy, but not crazy, giving him too much time to think about Kylie. Her image would pop into his mind at odd moments, making him wonder how she and Ben were doing.

Not his problem to worry about her son, but he couldn't seem to stop himself from thinking about Kylie anyway. He'd even run into Cheri, the new nurse from the second floor, in the cafeteria during his night shift, but although she'd been openly friendly with him, indicating she was interested, he hadn't asked her out as he'd originally planned.

Kylie Germaine was messing with his head, big-time.

He slept in on Sunday, and then prowled around his condo, searching for something to do to keep his mind off Kylie. Belatedly remembering his mother's box of family photos, which he and his siblings had found after her death, he hauled it into the living room and sat down to sift through them. The pictures of his smiling, happy parents, along with him and his older siblings at various birthday parties and holidays, made him feel sadly nostalgic.

And the sad memories only reinforced the very real reason why he avoided relationships.

They'd lost their father too young. After all these years he still missed him. Missed both his parents. The loss made his chest ache as he looked back over the happy moments captured on film. Even the family camping trips, with all the problems they'd tended to bring, had been fun.

Nothing could bring them back.

Sorting the photos into three stacks, trying to be fair as he divided up the pictures for himself and his siblings, wasn't easy. When he reached the bottom, however, he realized there was a piece of cardboard that didn't match the interior of the box covering something underneath. Using his pocket knife, he gently pried up the cardboard, revealing some fragile letters on pale blue paper, a marriage license, and a grainy black-and-white photograph.

The photograph was of his mother, wearing a knee-length white wedding dress, standing next to a strange guy in military uniform. With a deep frown he stared at the picture, trying to see if the man might be a younger version of his father. But the dark hair—his father had been a redhead—and the very different facial structure convinced him they weren't the same guy. He picked up the marriage license, shocked to discover his mother had gotten married to a man named Shane Andre the year before his oldest brother had been born.

What? How could that be? His father's name had been Gregory Taylor, not Shane Andre. Angry and confused, he sifted through the papers and found a death certificate for Shane Andre, issued by the United States Air Force. There was also a medal of honor, given post-humously in Shane Andre's name, for his bravery in attempting to save US hostages in Iran.

Stunned, he stared at the date of Shane Andre's death for a long time. The truth was staggering. He'd been born mere weeks before Shane's death. He, Tess and Caleb were all just one year apart in age. His mother had been married to Shane Andre for four years.

Which meant their biological father must have been Shane, not Gregory Taylor, as they'd believed all their lives.

Why on earth would their mother have lied to them? Why wouldn't she have told them the truth? With an angry swipe, he shoved the paperwork and photos aside and rose with an agitated lurch to his feet.

There was no reason he could think of to hide the truth. Why on earth would his mother keep such a big secret?

The angry pressure was building in his chest so he began to pace, taking slow, deep breaths.

There had to be a reason. His mother hadn't been a vengeful woman. The anger slowly eased, turning into a bewildered resentment. Had she kept the secret because it had been too painful to talk about her first husband?

He wished he knew. The marriage might have been brief but there had been three children born to the couple. He stopped and stared down at the grainy photograph, trying to comprehend what his mother's life had been like. She'd been a widow at a young age, with three small children to care for. He imagined the Air Force had provided some income for her, but when had she met their father, Gregory Taylor? It must have been shortly after their biological father's death.

He wanted to know the details. How exactly his parents had fallen in love. All he'd ever been told was that they'd met at a party given by mutual friends.

But he hadn't known his mother had been a widow at the time.

All his life he'd believed Gregory Taylor was his dad. But really his biological father was Shane Andre. A young pilot killed in the line of duty.

Damn. He scrubbed his hands over his face, knowing he needed to call Caleb and Tess, to tell them the news. He even reached for the phone, but then he stopped.

He couldn't do this now. Not yet. Not when he was still feeling so resentful. Not when he hadn't even really accepted the truth for himself.

Besides, Caleb and Tess were both busy with their respective families. Why make them miserable, too? His gaze rested on the small pack of pale blue letters. From the address on the top one he could see it was correspondence between his mother and Shane Andre.

He couldn't read them. Not now. Heck, maybe not ever. For some reason he couldn't quite accept that his mother hadn't been honest.

Had she planned to tell them at all?

Maybe. Her death had been sudden, the aneurysm in her brain bursting without warning. It wasn't as if she'd been sick for a while, knowing the end was near.

Yet on the other hand she'd had years to tell them the truth and hadn't.

He wished he could talk to Kylie. As an outsider, not part of the family, she might have a different perspective. Especially since she was a young single mother herself.

No. What was he thinking? Kylie wasn't like his mother. Kylie couldn't know why she'd kept the truth a secret. He was just using that as an excuse to talk to her. Despite his decision to stay away from her and Ben, he found he was looking forward to seeing her tomorrow at their meeting.

Strange to realize he had more in common with Kylie's son Ben than he'd originally thought.

Neither one of them knew the man who'd sired them.

Kylie swiped her damp palms on the sides of her pants, feeling unaccountably nervous about her scheduled meeting with Seth Taylor. She'd purposely worn her dark blue paramedic's uniform, since she'd been sorely tempted to wear something nice and feminine. Shaking her head at her own foolishness, she grabbed the hypothermia protocol she'd created, using the ones she'd researched as a template, and quickly headed out to her car. She drove the short distance to Cedar Bluff Hospital, nestled off the highway, just on the outskirts of the town.

The building didn't look much like a hospital, if you asked her. Most of the hospitals she'd been in had been huge white buildings. Not Cedar Bluff. This hospital was built on a hill, against the backdrop of a gently wooded area, the hospital's brown frame blending nicely with the landscape.

Peaceful. The first time she'd seen the hospital and the town she'd sensed she'd found a home. A great place to raise her son.

Ben was back in day care today, and the stitches over his eye seemed to be healing nicely. She'd made an appointment for Tuesday with the ophthalmologist, as Seth had suggested. Ben's school started in ten days, and she still had so much to do.

She parked in the ED parking lot and walked inside. Hoping Seth wouldn't be forced to cancel their meeting, she swept a glance through the trauma room, noting with relief the place didn't appear too busy. She stood for a minute in the center of the ED area, seeking a familiar face before she spotted him.

Her heart squeezed with an unfamiliar flash of jealousy when she saw him smiling down at one of the nurses, looking handsome, as always, with that stubborn lock of dark hair falling rakishly over his brow.

What on earth was wrong with her? What did she care who Seth Taylor smiled at?

Unfortunately she was still staring directly at him when he glanced in her direction, catching her eye. His smile deepened and he murmured something to the nurse without breaking eye contact, then headed straight toward her.

"Hi, Kylie," he greeted her cheerfully. "How are you?"

"I'm good, thanks." She inwardly cursed her heart for racing when he approached. She strove for a light tone. "I hope this is still a good time for us to meet?"

"You managed to arrive during a momentary lull," he said dryly. Lightly clasping her arm, he drew her toward his office, where they'd met before. "But I really hope you don't mind that I had lunch delivered. If you've already eaten, maybe you'll forgive my rudeness if I munch while we talk?"

His attitude was so matter-of-fact, how could she mind? The poor guy had to eat sometime. Maybe she'd overreacted to his asking her to meet over a meal. Doctors were much like paramedics—they had to grab food whenever the opportunity presented itself.

"How is Ben feeling?" Seth asked, as he opened the office door for her.

"He's fine."

"Good. I'm glad to hear it."

His tone was sincere, and it was nice of him to ask about Ben. Although Seth being a nice guy only made ignoring her physical reaction to him that much harder.

Keep it professional, she reminded herself.

His desk had been cleared to make room for two place settings and a plate of sandwiches in the middle. As an impromptu meal, everything looked very good. Her stomach rumbled, since she hadn't eaten anything except some cold cereal with Ben earlier that morning.

"What would you like to drink? Water? Or a soft drink?"

"Water is fine." Why did this suddenly feel like a date? She set the hypothermia protocol on the desk, as a tangible reminder that this was a business meeting.

"Here you go." Seth set a bottle of water in front of her and then sat down on the other side of the desk. He helped himself to a sandwich, taking a big bite, as if he were famished.

"Thanks." She took the water and took a quick sip to wet her suddenly dry throat. She handed him the papers she'd brought. "Here's a draft of a hypothermia protocol that I put together after researching what other institutions have been using. It might not be exactly what you're looking for, but I thought it would be a good starting point. I'm happy to make whatever changes you recommend."

"Excellent," Seth said with frank approval. He took another bite of his sandwich as he scanned her work. "This is great. We can probably use this protocol just as you've written it."

"Really?" Ridiculously pleased by his comment, she relaxed enough to help herself to a sandwich.

"Absolutely. From a medical perspective you have everything covered." He set the protocol aside and pulled out some paperwork of his own. "I've been working on the equipment side of things. I know the paramedic budget is tight, but I found a device the company will allow us to use for free if we buy their supplies." He handed her a picture of the hypothermia machine. "What do you think?"

The portable device was small enough to fit on the foot of a gurney, with a hypothermia blanket covering the patient from chin to toe. "Impressive," she murmured. "We'd need one for every unit, though."

"I have it covered," Seth assured her. His smile was dazzling, and she had to look away, reminding herself not to read too much into it. "All you need to do is to help me distribute the equipment to the paramedic units."

"I can do that," she agreed, without hesitation. "Once I get everyone trained on the device, that is."

"How long do you think that will take?" Seth asked, his dark brows pulling together in a slight frown.

She understood his frustration at the potential delay. She was just as eager to start with the new protocol as he was. "Our next quarterly educational update is in two weeks."

"Are you sure that's enough time?" He raised a skeptical brow. "You have to learn how to use the device yourself first, don't you?"

She nodded. "Yes, but I don't want to have to wait another three months, either. I'll contact this company today, to schedule the initial training. Do you think we can get a rush on the equipment delivery?"

"I'll do my best," Seth drawled. His gaze landed on her empty plate. "Please, help yourself to another sandwich."

She did as he suggested, figuring it was too late to protest now, after she'd already eaten one sandwich. They were delicious, and she wondered if he'd ordered them from the hospital cafeteria. If so, Cedar Bluff Hospital had better food than they'd offered at Chicago General.

Cedar Bluff was better than Chicago in more ways than one.

Amusement crinkled the corners of his eyes as he watched her eat. She felt her cheeks blush, and cursed her fair skin. "Thanks. I guess I was hungrier than I realized."

"You're welcome."

She was grateful he was enough of a gentleman not to remind her how much she'd protested against sharing a meal with him. When she'd finished her sandwich, she began gathering her things together.

"Kylie?"

She glanced at him. "Yes?"

"Have you made an appointment for Ben to see the ophthalmologist?"

She was a little disconcerted by the change in subject. "Yes, in fact we go in to see Dr. Greenley tomorrow."

"Will you let me know what Greenley says?"

"Sure." She didn't quite understand why Seth cared what the eye doctor had to say about Ben's vision. Maybe he was just being nice, making conversation about her son. They obviously didn't have anything else in common outside of work. "Actually, Ben has become quite obsessed about football ever since you put that orange-and-blue cast on his arm."

"I bet he'd love to play the game himself—once the cast comes off, that is."

She nodded. "Absolutely. I tried to find a football team for him to join, but I found out the peewee leagues have already started, and they'll be over before he gets his cast taken off." Ben had been very disappointed at the news. "But there's always next year. Especially now that I know how early they start. Ben will get over it, I'm sure."

"It's going to be hard keeping him entertained while he has that cast on," he said. "If you're not busy this weekend, there's a hospital employee baseball game on Saturday afternoon, at Cedar Bluff Park. The RNs challenge the MDs, and the game starts at one in the afternoon if you're interested in coming by to watch."

"That might be fun," she said, noncommittally. "Are you playing?"

"Yeah, I am."

She raised a skeptical brow. "If the doctors and nurses are playing, who's staffing the hospital?"

"We take turns—unless someone volunteers to work. Heck, some of our patients even come to watch us play." Seth flashed another of his lethal grins. "Did you think we'd close the hospital down for a baseball game?"

She flushed again and rose to her feet. "No, of course not."

Seth stood also, and then circled the desk to open the office door for her. He was so close she could smell the musky scent of his aftershave. The smell pleased her far more than it should.

"So you'll stop by? We could use some help in the cheering section. For some reason the nurses tend to get all the support around here."

His gaze was addictive, his nearness making her pulse leap again. For a moment she almost forgot what he was saying. Then she pulled herself together with an effort.

A baseball game. A family event. Nothing special. Certainly not something he wouldn't have hesitated to invite anyone to. Hadn't he just said the patients even joined the fun?

"Sure." Her house wasn't all that far from the park. And the game might help Ben take his mind off his broken arm. Her son was already starting to chafe at the restrictions. "We live so close to the park we can walk over to watch."

"Great." Seth's fingers brushed hers, and she told herself not to be an idiot—the touch was likely by accident. "I'll look forward to seeing you this weekend, then, if not before."

If not before? For a moment she didn't understand his comment, but then belatedly realized he meant he'd see her at work. When she brought in another patient to the ED, as she had the first day they'd met. It hadn't even been a full week since they'd taken care of their female heart attack patient together, and yet she already felt as if she'd known him much longer than that.

Her problem, not his. "Bye, Seth." She turned and walked away before she made a bigger fool of herself than she had already.

Seth was just being nice. Taking pity on a single mother with a young son who were new to the area and didn't know many people in the community yet.

Reading anything further into his casual invitation to watch the hospital baseball game was just asking for trouble.

CHAPTER FIVE

SETH didn't see Kylie again until Wednesday, toward the end of his shift. A page had come, regarding a motorcycle crash, and when she arrived with the patient a few minutes later he realized her unit must have been the first responder to the scene.

"Nineteen-year-old male with multiple contusions and road rash. Also has a right broken tibia."

Kylie spoke calmly and succinctly as she reported. He admired the way she kept her head in an emergency.

"We kept him on the long board to rule out back or neck injuries. He was wearing a helmet. He woke up during transport and has been answering questions appropriately."

From the extent of the road rash, he could see riding a motorcycle in shorts and a T-shirt wasn't smart. The guy was lucky he'd been wearing the helmet or he would have been in far worse shape. Seth stepped forward to take charge of the patient, although it seemed Kylie had things pretty much under control.

"All right, let's get a full set of labs and vital signs. Then get ready for a trip to the scanner."

"I suspect he might have a history of seizures," Kylie

murmured in a low undertone, as if she didn't want the patient to overhear. "When we arrived at the scene I thought for sure he looked postictal. But when I asked him about having a seizure disorder on the ride over he denied it."

He lifted a brow. "Hmm. I don't think he's supposed to be riding a motorcycle if he has a seizure disorder. And it makes me wonder if a seizure is what caused the crash," he mused. Turning to the nurse who held the numerous lab tubes in her hand, he added, "Make sure they run a full tox screen. I want to know if he has any medication in his system."

"Maybe this is a new onset of seizures?" Kylie asked with a perplexed frown.

"Not very likely. Although I guess anything is possible. I'll know more when we get his labs back."

Seth liked the way Kylie stayed around after bringing her patient into the ED. She didn't do a dump and run, like many of the other paramedics did. She made sure every aspect of the care was fully transferred over to the hospital staff and all questions answered before leaving.

They found the patient's ID and discovered his name was Dustin O'Malley. Seth knew the kid's parents—mostly because John O'Malley was in charge of the local hardware store and had helped Michael with some renovations on his house. He'd thought Dustin had gone off to college, but apparently the young man was home for the summer. He asked for Dustin's medical records to see what his history might be. Sure enough, Seth read that Dustin did have a well-documented seizure disorder.

Did his parents even realize he'd bought a motorcycle?

Dustin was lucky. He'd escaped without too serious an injury. But next time a seizure at the wrong moment could cost him his life.

Once Seth was satisfied that Dustin's vital signs were stable, he sent him off to get a CT scan of his entire body.

He checked on another patient while Dustin was in Radiology. When he returned to the trauma bay Kylie was loading the long board onto the paramedic gurney. Quickening his pace, he caught her arm before she could leave. "Hey, wait a minute. How did Ben's eye appointment go?"

She smiled, but he noticed her eyes were shadowed with worry. "The appointment was fine, except Dr. Greenley saw something that might be abnormal and he wants to make sure it doesn't get any worse. We have to go back for a follow-up visit in another week."

Something abnormal? Like maybe a detached retina? He'd been worried about that himself, it was no wonder she was concerned. "I'm sure he'll be fine," he reassured her. He almost offered to go with her to the follow-up appointment, but caught himself in the nick of time. What was he thinking? There was no reason for *him* to go to Ben's appointment. Bad enough he'd invited her and Ben to Saturday's game.

"Yes, he'll be fine," she repeated, although she didn't sound convinced.

He fought the insane urge to pull her into his arms. The day of their lunch meeting he'd been tempted to kiss her. There was something about Kylie that had gotten under his skin. He needed to get his inappropriate physical reaction to her under control, and fast.

"Well, if you need something let me know."

She looked surprised by his offer, and he inwardly cursed, realizing he wasn't doing a very good job of hiding his feelings.

In the past it had always been easy to keep women at arm's length. So why this strange urge to force himself into Kylie's life?

Before she could respond, Nanette Drake, a pretty paramedic with bright red hair, whom he'd dated a couple of times in the past, came up and put a casual arm around his waist in a half hug. "Hey, Romeo, long time no see. How are you?"

"Romeo?" Kylie echoed with an arched brow.

Damn. He really detested that nickname. It had been started by an ICU nurse, Rachel, who'd been upset by his no-strings rule. Showing his aversion to the nickname, however, would only encourage people to use it more. So he kept his mouth shut, although it wasn't easy.

Especially now, beneath Kylie's slightly accusing stare.

"Romeo because our Seth Taylor has quite the reputation with the ladies," Nanette teased.

He knew Nanette wasn't being purposefully mean, but he wished she'd shut up.

"Oh, really?" Kylie murmured, taking a step back, as if she wanted to leave.

"No. Not really. Nanette likes to exaggerate." He glanced away, not wanting Kylie to see the truth in his eyes. He'd never apologized for being who he was, and he didn't intend to start now. No matter how much it irritated him to have Kylie thinking the worst.

His pager went off, announcing the arrival of another patient. "Excuse me, ladies, I need to go. I'll see you Saturday, Kylie. Nanette, don't tell her too many unflattering stories about me."

"Only the true ones," Nanette promised with a laugh.

He scowled, seeing the withdrawal in Kylie's eyes moments before she turned away to head back out to the paramedic rig.

Yeah. Only the true ones. That was exactly what he was afraid of.

"Seth is a nice guy, but not the kind of man you want to get involved with," Nanette said as they loaded their gear inside the ambulance. "He's the type who plays the field, never getting serious about one woman."

"I'm not looking to get involved," Kylie said, desperately trying to think of a way to change the subject. She really, *really* didn't want to hear the details of what had transpired between Nanette and Seth. "After my son Ben's father left, I learned it was better not to count on anyone but myself."

"Ben's father ran off on you?" Nanette's sympathetic gaze caught hers. "What a jerk."

Kylie shrugged. What could she say? Tristan *had* been a jerk. "I'm over it. Honestly I'd rather be alone than have to share custody of Ben with some guy who'd resent every moment."

"I can certainly understand that. And I give you credit," Nanette said. "It can't be easy raising a child alone."

No, it wasn't easy. But since she'd moved to Cedar Bluff her worry ratio had diminished considerably. After the horrible crime she'd experienced firsthand in Chicago, the nice, laid-back atmosphere of the town was perfect for them. Even the hospital had a calmer atmosphere than Chicago General. There were still times late at night when she'd wake up, her heart pounding from the all too familiar nightmare, but all she had to do was to open her window and gaze up at the stars, fill her head with the scent of fresh clean air and she felt better.

Even considering Ben's recent accident with his bike, she was glad she'd made the move.

She didn't need a man in her life. All she needed was a safe, secure place to raise her child. And, luckily for her, Ben had adapted to their new home with an easy flexibility.

Thankfully, Nanette dropped the subject of Seth as they made their way back to base. Still, their interaction at the hospital lingered in her mind. Romeo. It just figured the first guy she'd been attracted to since Tristan left would have to be a man who'd earned the nickname Romeo. Which was exactly why she needed to stay away from him.

Nanette had hugged Seth with the familiarity of old friends, but clearly her partner had spent some time with Seth on a personal basis. She had no reason to doubt Nanette's claim that Seth was known for dating lots of women and committing to none. Hadn't she sensed the same thing about him after their first meeting?

Better to know the truth now than to find out later, once she was emotionally involved. Seth was exactly the type of guy she needed to avoid.

She'd promised to go to the baseball game and she would—but only because Ben would enjoy the outing. She'd be polite to Seth. Friendly. She could certainly use friends as she built a new life for herself and for Ben here in Cedar Bluff.

Satisfied with her decision, Kylie used her downtime between patient runs to work on setting up a demonstration of the hypothermia machine.

Work helped to keep her focused on what was important.

The following Saturday, Kylie realized she'd underestimated the appeal of the annual hospital baseball game. Cedar Bluff Park was jam-packed with people. If she and Ben hadn't walked the short distance from her house they would never have found a parking space.

As it was, the game was already underway as she and Ben found seats on the doctors' side of the bench. She sat next to a woman named Marla—her daughter, Raelynn, and Ben were in the same day care center. After exchanging quick greetings, she turned her attention to the game. The nurses must have been first up at bat, because they were already winning two to nothing.

She'd never figure out how Seth had managed to pick her and Ben out of the crowd, but shortly after she and Ben got settled in their seats he jogged over to greet them.

He looked great. Better than great. Wonderful. Sexy.

Her heart stumbled in her chest, and she had to look away so he wouldn't see the stark longing in her gaze.

Romeo, she reminded herself. Seth wasn't interested

in relationships. He wasn't there to see her. He was just being nice.

Friendly.

"Hi, Kylie, Ben." Seth wore a bright blue T-shirt that said "MD" on the back. The nurses were in matching red shirts with "RN" on the back. "Glad you could make it."

"I said we would," she responded, trying not to sound defensive. "And you told me the nurses always got more support." She swept a skeptical glance over the packed sidelines. "I'd say the support is about even."

"The crowd is larger than last year," Seth admitted. He caught her gaze with his. "Will you and Ben wait for me after the game? There's a whole group of us going out for pizza afterwards."

"Yeah, Mom. *Pizza!*" Ben shouted with glee.

She silently damned him for asking in front of Ben. If she declined, she'd be the bad guy, left to explain to a six-year-old why they couldn't go. The last thing she wanted to do right now was to spend more time with Seth. But at the same time she couldn't remember the last time Ben had been so excited. A friendly gathering after the game would hardly be personal if everyone else was going, too.

She finally relented, unwilling to disappoint Ben. "Sure. I guess."

"Great." Seth's gaze flared with pleasure, despite her less than enthusiastic tone, and warning bells went off in her mind, making her shift uncomfortably in her seat. Why did she suddenly feel as if she'd accepted an invitation to go out on a date with him? Marla's quick smile didn't help her feel any better. Cedar Bluff wasn't exactly a big place. Surely the rumors would start buzzing if she was seen out with Seth? Just what she didn't need.

Vowing to make sure she sat by someone else, she almost didn't hear him say, "I'll see you after the game, then."

"Sure. Good luck." She shadowed her eyes with her hand as Seth jogged back over to the dugout.

"He's next up at bat, Mom," Ben pointed out, as Seth picked up a bat and took several practice swings.

"I see him, Ben." She wished she didn't. Because watching Seth's backside as he waited for the pitch was a little too intriguing.

The pitcher—one of the nurses who'd managed to strike out the first batter—took her time, as if attempting to psych Seth out. Finally she threw the ball and Seth swung at the first pitch, hitting the ball dead center with a loud crack, sending it sailing over the nurses' heads. The nurses in the backfield took off running, but their efforts were in vain as the ball flew well out of their range.

Ben shouted at the top of his lungs as Seth ran the bases. Seth flashed them a cheeky grin and waved as he ran past the third base marker, then slid into home with a flourish.

The nurses' side of the bench groaned, while the physicians' side cheered.

"A home run! Did you see that, Mom?" Ben's voice was full of awe. "Dr. Seth hit a home run."

"I saw it," she replied absently. Unfortunately she couldn't seem to tear her gaze away from him as Seth's teammates congratulated him with a series of high fives and he headed toward the dugout.

He went down into the dugout, disappearing from view and breaking the invisible hold he had on her. Taking a deep breath, she swallowed hard. She was in trouble. Deep trouble. She liked Seth. Too much.

Staring at her feet, she tried to think of a way to get out of the post-game pizza party. As much as she didn't want to disappoint Ben, she needed to protect herself.

She'd been alone for a long time. Any man's attention would probably make her feel this way. Maybe she needed a fling with some other guy? Someone who could take her mind off a certain rather athletic ED physician.

Ben was oblivious to her discomfort as he continued to loudly cheer for Seth's team.

The game was tied at the bottom of the last inning. Still seated on the doctors' side of the bench, Kylie found she was impressed at how well the nurses held their own—especially when men dominated the physician players. Beside her, Marla was rooting almost as loudly as Ben, and she soon figured out her husband must be on Seth's team.

Seth was up at bat again, and the nurses' team had sent in a relief pitcher to give the previous one a break. He stood in the batter's box, waiting for the pitch. The first ball went way wide, nowhere near his bat, so he didn't swing. The pitcher tried again. This time her pitch went wild in the opposite direction, heading straight for Seth. He ducked to avoid getting hit, but too late.

Kylie heard a loud *thunk* as the ball hit him, the sound carrying all the way to her seat. For a long moment he stood there, but then slowly sank to his knees, his hand cradling his head.

Her heart jumped into her throat.

One minute he was thinking about slamming the ball over the back fence to win the game, and the next he was lying flat on his back, staring up at the sunny sky.

His jaw throbbed. Seth squinted against the brightness, gradually remembering what had happened. Rachel's second pitch had gone wild, smacking him in the face.

Rachel also just happened to be the nurse who'd gifted him the Romeo moniker. Had she hit him on purpose? Nah, he didn't really think so. Pushing aside the well-meaning doctors and nurses who'd gathered around, he sat up, gingerly sliding his jaw back and forth. Man, he hoped nothing was broken. Like his mandible or his teeth.

"Seth? My gosh, are you all right?"

Kylie's earnest expression was a little fuzzy as she hovered over him, but knowing she'd rushed to his side when he was injured made him want to smile. If his face hadn't hurt so much, that was. "Fine," he said in a gruff tone, embarrassed by all the attention.

He'd have felt better if he'd gotten smacked *after* hitting a game-winning home run.

She helped him upright, and damned if he didn't feel a little dizzy. He tried to brush off the sensation, but as he took a step found himself leaning against Kylie.

He heard the umpire making arrangements for a pinch hitter to take his place. He wanted to protest—because, darn it, *he'd* wanted to be the one to score the win.

"Just sit down here for a minute," Kylie was saying, as she led him down the few steps into the shaded area of the dugout.

"I'm fine," he said, taking the seat farthest away at the end, to stay out of the other players' way. "I just feel stupid—like I should have been able to avoid getting hit."

"Why? Because you think you're Superman or some-thing?" she asked in an exasperated tone.

He didn't notice who'd taken his turn at bat. He was too focused on Kylie. In her casual clothes, jeans and a tight-fitting short-sleeved shirt, she looked beautiful. "You mean I'm not?" he said lightly.

"No." She took a cold pack out of the first aid kit and placed it against his jaw, kneeling in front of him where he sat on the bench. Her face was tipped up toward his, and he thought the touch of her slender hand felt much better than any ice pack. Her eyes were full of concern. "You scared me to death when you went down."

"I'm sorry." He couldn't seem to tear his gaze away from her luscious mouth. One taste. All he wanted was one taste of her lips.

Whoever had taken his turn at bat must have hit a good one, because suddenly the dugout emptied as the MD players jumped to their feet, loudly cheering.

He ignored them. So did Kylie. She stared up at him, and suddenly he couldn't help himself. He leaned forward and captured her mouth in a sweet, intoxicating kiss.

The moment her mouth parted for his he knew he'd lied. Because one taste of Kylie would never be enough.

CHAPTER SIX

KYLIE dropped the cold pack and clutched Seth's shoulders, surprised and then enthralled by his kiss. His mouth was firm, yet gentle, sensual, but very masculine, as he deepened the kiss. Every nerve in her body yearned for his touch, and helplessly she leaned in, exploring his mouth with a keen intensity.

Everything faded away except the two of them.

Dear heaven, she wanted him. Wanted more. Wanted everything he had to offer. There was a reason she'd tried to avoid this, but at the moment she couldn't think of it.

And then it hit her. *Ben.* Cripes, what was wrong with her? She'd run off to see if Seth was all right, and had completely forgotten her son.

She broke the kiss, yanked out of Seth's embrace, and scrambled awkwardly to her feet. What kind of mother was she that she forgot her own son?

The baseball game was over. She climbed from the dugout, catching a glimpse of the large scoreboard to see the MDs had taken the lead with that last run. Spectators streamed down from the bleachers and Kylie frantically pushed against them, searching wildly for the spot where she'd left her son.

"Ben? Where are you? Ben!"

Surprisingly, Seth had followed her, his deep voice booming above hers, helping her to call her son. "Ben. *Ben!*"

"Mom?"

Miraculously she spotted him, holding on to his playmate Raelynn's hand. She in turn was hanging on to her mother's. Relief swept over her as she rushed forward, making her way as quickly as she could against the mob of people vying to go in the opposite direction.

"Ben!" She enveloped him in a bone-crushing hug. Her apologetic gaze caught Marla's. "I'm sorry. I shouldn't have left you like that. I'm *so* sorry."

"It's okay," Marla responded, surprisingly calm and not the least bit annoyed. "I knew we'd find you eventually. Besides, I was waiting for Eric to find *us*. He's one of the OB doctors on the MD team."

She closed her eyes, realizing that she'd overreacted and willing her rioting fear to settle down. Ben was safe. Cedar Bluff wasn't Chicago. Cedar Bluff was safe.

She didn't have to relive the fear of the past anymore.

"Dr. Seth!" Ben exclaimed, looking past her to where Seth stood. "Did you get hurt?"

"I'm fine, Ben," he reassured him. "I wasn't hurt nearly as bad as you were the day that car hit you."

Kylie was glad Ben didn't seem to be upset by her disappearance. And she was grateful her son hadn't witnessed the kiss. She forced herself to relax and take

Ben's hand, even though she knew there was no way she could now go to the post-game party with Seth.

Not after the way she'd practically drowned in his kiss.

Not after the way she'd almost lost her son.

She turned toward Seth. "I'm sorry, but I don't think we're up for that post-game pizza after all." She was babbling, but somehow couldn't make herself stop. When her son's face fell, she added, "Ben, we'll make frozen pizza at home, all right?"

"Aw, Mom," Ben protested. "I wanna go to the party."

His dejected expression almost made her change her mind.

Almost.

"I'm not in the mood for a party, either," Seth admitted, fingering the bruise that was just starting to darken the skin along his jaw. "Do you mind if I come with you instead? Pizza at home sounds like heaven at the moment."

"Cool," Ben piped up.

"Yes. No. I mean—sure." Flustered, she agreed, not wanting to sound rude, and unable to think of a graceful way out. Helplessly she shrugged. "If you really want to."

"I do." His gaze bored into hers, as if he knew full well she'd been trying to get away from him. "Thanks."

So Seth was coming over to her house. Fine. He'd been there before, when he'd driven her and Ben home from the hospital after Ben's accident. She'd just have to feed him pizza and then shoo him out.

She swiped suddenly damp palms on the seat of her jeans and glanced around, realizing with relief that the crowd had thinned. "We—uh—walked here from the house."

"No problem. I'll walk back with you." Seth fell into step beside her, but then stopped. "Wait, I almost forgot my gear—my bat and glove. Will you give me a quick minute?"

"Of course." What did he think? That she'd take off the second his back was turned? Tempting, but she wasn't that much of a coward. Well, maybe she was. But she still refused to give in to the cowardly thought, regardless.

"Can I come with you?" Ben asked. "I'll carry your glove."

"Absolutely. As long as your Mom says it's okay."

"Go ahead," she said, forcing a smile. "I'll wait for you both here."

Ben eagerly turned toward Seth. As if Seth had read her mind, he held out his hand. "Grab on, so I don't lose you in the crowd."

Ben took Seth's hand with his non-casted one.

Her throat tightened as she watched the two of them walk hand in hand to the dugout, where Seth had accidentally left his equipment. She couldn't hear what Ben was saying, but Seth was nodding, listening intently to her son. As much as she hated to admit it, Seth would make a great father someday.

Not a good husband, perhaps, but a great father.

Tristan had seemed to be a good potential husband, yet had turned out to be a lousy father.

She rubbed a weary hand over her eyes. Somehow she needed to find a man who could be both.

Or, better still, stay single until Ben was old enough to go off to college.

* * *

Seth knew Kylie was anxiously waiting for him and Ben to return, but he needed a few minutes to get himself under control.

Kissing her had caused his hormones to play laser tag with his emotions. When she'd broken away from him it had taken several seconds for the sensual haze to clear, and then he'd figured out that Kylie was running away.

Never had a woman gotten to him so fast. Especially not a woman with a son. He'd realized Kylie was desperately searching for Ben when she'd taken off so abruptly.

The mere memory of their kiss still had the potency to make his blood heat. And it wasn't as if he'd kissed her in a private place. Oh, no, he'd chosen the romantic aura of the dugout to kiss her. He didn't think anyone else had noticed, though, since Michael had hit the game-winning home run.

"Can I wear your glove?" Ben asked, sliding his blue-and-orange casted hand into the palm of his large leather glove. Even despite the bulky cast, the mitt slipped drunkenly to one side on his tiny fist.

"Sure, but be careful you don't drop it." He didn't really care if Ben dropped the mitt or not. He was still too busy trying to figure out what had happened between him and Kylie in the dugout.

Okay, so it was possible that kissing her hadn't been the smartest idea he'd ever had. But, smart or not, he wanted nothing more than to kiss her again.

Which was why he'd boldly invited himself to her house after she'd begged off the pizza outing. Talk about being a glutton for punishment.

"Idiot," he muttered under his breath.

"Who's an idiot?" Ben asked.

He let out his breath in a heavy sigh. "No one. Sorry. I was thinking about something else." Kissing Kylie broke every no-strings rule he possessed. She was a mother with a son. Unless it was possible Kylie wasn't looking for anything serious, either? Warming to the idea, he reached for the boy's non-casted hand. "Come on, let's go back to meet your mom."

He and Kylie needed to talk. Soon. That electrifying kiss they'd shared had convinced him they couldn't ignore the desire simmering between them.

And maybe they could have a little fun without risking a full-blown relationship? Because he still wanted her. Not that he expected Kylie to end up in his bedroom on a casual whim. But it would be better if the rules were clear up front.

"Mom, Seth's glove almost fits me—see?" Ben ran the few feet necessary to catch up to Kylie, carrying the oversize glove on his casted hand.

"Wow, that's amazing. I bet that glove will fit you perfectly in a couple of years," Kylie gallantly agreed. She seemed to be avoiding Seth's gaze, though, keeping her attention centered on her son.

"Seth said I can carry it for him if I don't drop it."

"Don't you mean *Dr.* Seth?" she corrected gently.

"Yeah. That's what I said. Dr. Seth." Ben skipped ahead of them on the sidewalk, clearly not getting what his mother meant.

Seth lengthened his stride to catch up with her. "It's okay, I don't mind."

"I know, but that's not the point." Kylie was walking fast, as if she were on a marathon mission to get home. "He needs to respect his elders."

He cocked a brow, striving for a light tone. "Isn't that an old-fashioned view in this day and age?"

"Not as far as I'm concerned." Kylie still refused to look directly at him. "Good game, by the way. Although I don't think it's really fair how the MDs have so many men on the team compared to the nurses."

Ben wasn't far enough ahead for a private conversation, so he played along, keeping things light. "Obviously you can't count very well. There were at least five guys on the RN team. We had four women on ours, including Leila, who is a great trauma surgeon but doesn't have an athletic bone in her body. Didn't you notice she dropped every ball the nurses hit in her direction? Heck, we were almost perfectly matched."

"Oh, please!" she scoffed. "Each team had eleven players. Obviously you can't count very well."

He chuckled, liking the way she jumped to defend the underdogs. They'd been actually trying to even out the teams, but the nurses didn't seem to mind. Every year they continued to issue the challenge. "Yeah, but that Rachel packs a powerful punch. I mean pitch."

Kylie finally turned to look at him, frowning when her gaze landed on his bruised jaw. "Are you sure you're okay?"

Damn, the caring concern in her eyes made him want to kiss her again. And now Ben was far enough away that he could speak his mind. "Yes. And you should know—your kiss completely healed my pain."

Her eyes widened and she quickly turned away. "I don't know why you're so anxious to come and eat frozen pizza," she said abruptly, changing the subject. "Di Vinci's Pizza is much better."

"I don't care about the pizza." He decided he'd had enough of her light and fluffy conversation. They'd come abreast of her house anyway—he recognized it from the other day, when he'd given her a ride home. He caught her hand to stop her. "Kylie, there's a sizzling attraction between us. Why are you pretending it doesn't exist?"

She sucked in a harsh breath and tugged against his hand. "Don't," she said softly. "Don't do this."

"Do what?"

"Make me fall for you."

The seriousness of her tone made him drop her arm and take a step back. "Okay, that's fine. Neither one of us is looking for a long-term relationship. Does that mean we can't have any fun?"

Her gaze narrowed. "Fun? That kiss was a mistake. I'm sorry if I gave you the wrong impression. Now, if you really want pizza you're welcome to join us, but only as friends."

Disappointment burned as she yanked out of his grip and hurried up the driveway after her son. "Ben, why don't you talk to Dr. Seth while I put the pizza in the oven?"

He sighed and tried to smile. Clearly this wasn't going to work. But at the same time he couldn't just leave. At least not without hurting Ben. And, besides, he didn't mind spending time with the boy. Ben was eager to talk sports—one of his favorite subjects.

So instead of making a polite excuse to leave he

stayed, and entertained Ben while enjoying every bite of the pizza and garlic bread she'd made.

When the meal was over, he insisted on doing cleanup duty, while Kylie and Ben went into the living room to relax.

At least he assumed Ben was relaxing. Kylie had seemed tense throughout dinner. He suspected she'd remain tense until he went home.

Alone.

Dammit.

Kylie surprised him by returning to the kitchen a few minutes later. "Seth, really. You don't have to do this."

"Where's Ben?" he asked, continuing to wash the dishes. Her modest home didn't have the luxury of a dishwasher.

"He's watching some football game on television." She wrinkled her nose. "Someday I'm going to have to learn the finer points of that game."

"I'd be happy to teach you," he offered, before he could stop himself. "Ben's probably watching a college game—they're generally on Saturdays. The professionals play every Sunday."

"Hmm." She picked up a towel and began drying the dishes he'd stacked in the sink. "I should take you up on that."

"Football was always a big game at our house," he explained. "My dad used to coach our high school team. My oldest brother Caleb was a better player than I was, and my sister Tess was a cheerleader. We always spent every single Sunday watching the game on television, no exceptions."

Kylie smiled. "Your mother must have been a saint to put up with all of you watching football."

"Nah, she didn't mind so much. Honestly, I think she learned to love the game, too. Maybe just because my dad did." Seth finished washing and rinsing the dishes and took the towel from her hands to dry his own. Instead of giving it back, he took over the task of drying dishes. "When my dad died, the summer before my junior year of high school, we were pretty shocked. Caleb had already been accepted into college, but he tried to back out. Mom wouldn't hear of it. She insisted he go. So he compromised by changing the campus he'd planned to attend so he'd be closer to home. Tess and I went back to high school in the fall, but it wasn't the same without him."

Kylie's hand lightly rested on his arm. "That must have been hard for you, losing your father so young. Especially since he was such a big part of your life."

"It was. But we hung together, and Mom was great. When she died unexpectedly six months ago…" He shook his head. "That was almost worse, because she was pretty much the rock that had held us together."

"Oh, Seth." Kylie's eyes softened with empathy. "I'm so sorry."

He tried to smile. "Yeah. I loved her. But I'm also a little ticked at her. Because after going through a box of family photos I discovered my dad—the one who died when I was in high school—wasn't really my biological father after all."

"What? Are you sure?" Kylie looked shocked.

"Yeah, I'm sure." He finished drying the dishes and

tossed the damp towel on the counter. "And I don't like being angry at my mother, especially when she's not here to defend herself, but I am."

"How do you know he wasn't your father?"

"Because I found a wedding picture and a marriage certificate for my mom and an Air Force pilot named Shane Andre. He died a few weeks after I was born."

Her mouth formed a small O. "And you never knew?"

"No. I never knew. Throughout my whole life I believed Gregory Taylor was my father." He struggled to keep the bitterness out of his tone.

"My gosh. Your stepfather must have adopted you, since your last name is Taylor, but I wonder why your mother chose to keep it a secret?" Kylie asked, her brows puckering together in a slight frown.

"I don't know." He stared at her for a moment. "You're a single mother, like my mom was. What have you told Ben about *his* father? Does he know the truth?"

She paled and took a step back, looking distressed. "No, he doesn't know the truth. Not really. But it isn't the same situation at all."

He couldn't help looking grim, because to him it felt the same. "You mean you're not ever going to tell Ben the truth?"

Her gaze narrowed, and her voice practically shimmered with anger. "Don't you dare pass judgment on me," she hissed in a low voice. "Will I tell him the truth? Probably not. But it's not as if Ben's father died in a plane crash—a situation clearly beyond his control. Ben's father walked out, abandoning his own son before he was born. Do you really expect me to tell a six-year-old that his father left the moment I went into labor, leaving me all alone without a birthing coach?"

Her tone rose in agitation and he sent a worried glance toward the kitchen door, hoping Ben wouldn't come in.

"Those hours of labor were awful, and then the doctor told me Ben was breech and would need to be delivered via C-section. Which only worried me more. But I didn't have anyone to talk to. No one to comfort me as I went through surgery, praying my baby would be all right."

Her voice was literally shaking, and he felt like a jerk for upsetting her. He reached for her, but she hastily stepped away, wincing as she bumped her hip hard against the kitchen counter. "Kylie, I'm sorry. You're right. It's not the same thing at all."

"No, it's not." She wrapped her arms over her stomach, as if she were cold. As if it weren't a nice, breezy seventy-five degrees outside.

"I'm sorry," he said again, trying to ease closer, anxious to offer comfort. "I had no idea what he did to you."

"Yeah, well. Now you do." Kylie bravely lifted her chin and met his gaze head-on. "And now you understand why this isn't going to work. I'm not in a position to forget all my troubles, go out and have a little fun. I can't depend on anyone but myself. Not when it comes to Ben."

He disagreed. She shouldn't have to do everything alone. But this wasn't the time to argue. She was hurt, and he longed to make her feel better. He took another step closer and lightly reached for her, keeping his touch gentle and nonthreatening. "I think you're a wonderful mother to Ben."

She relaxed a bit and gave a tiny nod. "Thank you."

"I'm sorry. I didn't mean to make you so upset." He lightly stroked his hands up and down her arms. "Ben is very lucky to have you."

"And you were lucky to have your parents, too. Remember that whatever reason your mother had for not telling you the truth she loved you. And so did the man who adopted you as his own."

Gregory Taylor *had* adopted him. All three of them. He had raised them as his own.

Kylie was right. Being angry was stupid.

Especially when he was close enough to breathe in her sultry scent, her soft skin warming beneath his hands. He didn't want to hurt her, yet at the same time he couldn't stop himself from leaning down to brush another kiss across her luscious mouth.

"Seth…" she whispered.

"Shh," he soothed, drawing her closer. "Just a kiss, Kylie. Please?"

She lifted her head, stared into his eyes, and then raised up on her tiptoes to press her mouth against his.

CHAPTER SEVEN

UNABLE to deny something she wanted so desperately, Kylie fitted her mouth to his, kissing Seth even though she knew she was playing with fire.

But she hadn't been held by a man in a really long time. She'd been so cold and lonely. There was no way she could voluntarily tear herself away from Seth's welcoming heat.

His mouth hungrily slanted over hers, and she met his caress with an eager response of her own. The passion between them sizzled, like water droplets dancing in hot oil. The only difference between this kiss and the one during the baseball game was that it was Seth who ended the embrace.

"Kylie," he whispered in a hoarse tone as he rested his forehead against hers. "This is starting to feel complicated."

Complicated? Was that a good thing or a bad thing? The haze of desire clouding her senses made it difficult to think. Probably a bad thing. "Uh, okay."

He sighed and muttered a curse. "No, it's not okay. But it doesn't matter. Can I see you tomorrow?"

Tomorrow? Sunday? She knew she probably should say no, but her mouth answered before her brain could protest. "Sure."

"Good. That's good. I'll teach you about football as we watch the game." His tone was casual, but his gaze was intense. He might have been the one to step back, remembering better than she how Ben was just in the other room, but his dark brown eyes were almost black with banked desire.

"Great." She gathered her scattered thoughts, stifling a flash of disappointment that he hadn't asked her out for a proper date. Although hadn't she just told him she wasn't in the market for fun? The heat of his kiss had confused everything.

With Ben here, she wouldn't have to worry about any more toe-curling kisses. "I'll think of something to throw together for dinner."

"I was thinking we could go out for dinner—if you can find a babysitter for Ben? If not, he's welcome to join us."

She sucked in a breath. Did she dare go out with Seth on a real date? Maybe she was wrong to react so harshly? Would a little fun hurt? After everything she'd been through in the past year, she probably needed some fun.

"It's just a date, Kylie," Seth said when she hesitated.

She slowly nodded. "All right. I'm sure I can find a babysitter." There was a young girl who lived not far away who'd tucked a flyer in her mailbox shortly after they'd moved in, offering "reasonable rates" for baby-sitting services. Missy Clairmont had used the teenager a few times, and when she'd come over to apologize again after Ben's accident, she'd highly recommended Elise Eberson as a babysitter.

"Excellent," Seth murmured. He stepped back with a reluctant smile. "I'd better say good-night to Ben."

She wished she could ask him to stay, but that was one line she didn't dare cross, so she held her tongue as she followed him into the living room.

"Hey, Ben, I need to get going. But I'll stop by and watch the game with you tomorrow," he said in a cheerful tone.

"Cool!" Ben tore his gaze away from the game to grin widely up at Seth.

"You know we'll have to watch the Packers game, not necessarily the Chicago Bears game," Seth pointed out. "Depending on if the Bears play later, it might be broadcast on TV. But the bigger question is, are you sure you can handle the pressure if the Packers win?"

"I can handle it," Ben said with confidence. "Go Bears!"

Seth chuckled and lightly ruffled Ben's hair. "Go Packers. See you tomorrow, Ben."

"Bye, Dr. Seth."

Ben's easy acceptance of Seth's plan to return the next day caused a tiny niggle of worry to work its way under her skin. She ignored the sensation as she walked Seth to the front door.

He caught her hand and gave it a slight squeeze. "See you tomorrow, Kylie."

She tried to smile. "Good night, Seth."

When he left, she was keenly aware of his absence.

Maybe it wasn't Ben's easy acceptance of Seth's

plan to return the next day she should worry about but her own. She leaned against the closed door for a moment, fighting the sudden doubts.

Why was she doing this? Hadn't she decided Seth couldn't be anything more than a friend? Why had she agreed to see him again?

Yet instinctively she trusted that Seth would never hurt Ben. Not the way Tristan had, walking away when her baby's life had literally been in danger.

Shaking her head at her own foolishness, and her inability to keep her distance from Seth, she pushed away from the door and headed back toward the kitchen. Where had she put that babysitter's phone number?

The next day, Seth arrived at a quarter to twelve, just fifteen minutes before the game was scheduled to start. He wore a bright green Packers jersey and tossed Ben a small bag. "This is for you. I hope you like it."

Ben eagerly opened the bag, letting out a whoop of joy. "A Bears jersey!" he said excitedly. He pulled out the navy blue football shirt with the bright orange numbers on the front and yanked it over his head, grinning from ear to ear even though the jersey almost hung to his knees. "Thanks, Seth."

"*Dr.* Seth," Kylie corrected with a smile. It was nice of Seth to bring something for Ben. The idea of buying Ben a football jersey had never occurred to her. Trust Seth to think like a young boy.

She carried out some snacks, chips and dip for them to munch on during the game, and when Seth patted the seat on the sofa next to him sank down beside him.

He was close enough to touch, but she left a good six inches of space between them, trying not to start every time he lightly brushed against her. He flashed her that sexy grin as he began outlining the basic instructions of the game. She listened intently, watching as the play unfolded on the television. Soon she realized the game wasn't nearly as complicated as she'd originally thought.

Each team had four chances to gain ten yards, with the ultimate goal being to get the football inside the other team's end zone.

Simple, really.

But as the game progressed she discovered there were lots of confusing rules. Why they had to make such picky rules was beyond her. From what she could tell, the men on the front line were *always* holding, not just those few times the referee threw a yellow flag to penalize the team. And why did all the guys on the line rush toward the kicker if they couldn't hit him? Some rules just didn't make sense.

Her gaze landed on Ben, and she frowned when she noticed he was watching the game holding his head at an odd angle.

"Ben, what's wrong with your neck?" she asked.

"Nothing." He didn't turn to look at her, but took another chip doused with shrimp dip.

"Then why are you sitting with your head tilted like that?" she persisted, exchanging a worried glance with Seth.

"So I can see better."

Seth frowned. "Is the television blurry?"

"A little," he admitted.

Seth got off the sofa and crossed over to where Ben was sitting on the floor. "Look at me," he commanded.

Ben obediently turned, so he was facing Seth.

"Hold up your hand to cover your left eye," Seth instructed. Ben's left eye was the one with the stitches. "How blurry am I now?"

"You're not blurry at all," Ben said.

Seth nodded. "Okay, cover up your right eye instead. Now how blurry am I?"

"Really blurry. There's, like, two of you."

Kylie sucked in a breath, trying not to panic when Seth's concerned gaze met hers.

"I think you'd better give that ophthalmologist a call."

"I will." Kylie rose to her feet and headed for the kitchen where she'd kept her appointment book. Ben had a follow-up appointment with Dr. Greenley on Tuesday, but she suspected her son needed to be seen sooner.

She dialed the number listed on Geoff Greenley's card, but as it was a Sunday she was routed through to his answering service. She left a message, including her home phone number and her cell phone number, before hanging up.

After taking a deep breath, she let it out slowly. There was nothing more she could do right now except wait.

She turned back toward the living room, then paused and glanced back at the phone. If Ben was having trouble with his vision she'd need to cancel Elise, the babysitter, too.

Stifling a pang of regret, Kylie reached for the phone. It was probably for the best anyway, because after two sizzling kisses her emotions were already too tangled up in Seth for her own good.

Seth wanted to have fun. He hadn't made any promises. She never should have agreed to go out with him. She knew it was all too possible he'd eventually get bored and move on to the next woman, like he always did.

Potentially leaving her heart shattered in a million broken pieces once he was gone.

Seth drove Kylie and Ben to the hospital, irked to realize that as the afternoon wore on, while they'd waited for Dr. Greenley to call back, Kylie had once again distanced herself from him.

He understood she was worried about Ben. After everything she'd been through with Ben's father she was clearly used to handling crises alone, and with the ominous changes in her son's vision she had a right to be concerned.

Still, he didn't think Ben was the only reason she was practically ignoring him. Something else had happened to make her retreat, and darned if he could pinpoint what he'd done.

He hadn't even kissed her—even though he'd thought of little else during the afternoon. The football game hadn't held his attention like Kylie.

They'd arranged to meet Dr. Greenley in the ED. It was odd coming into the department as a patient's family member rather than as part of the staff.

"Hey, Seth." Simon Carter, the ED physician he'd covered for the previous weekend greeted him when they walked in. His curious gaze rested on Kylie and Ben. "Hi, Kylie. What's wrong? Is there something you need?"

"We're actually meeting Dr. Greenley here, to check out Ben's left eye." He quickly introduced Kylie's son. "Do you have an empty room for us?"

"Sure thing. Although I think you bypassed Registration." Simon grinned as he gestured for them to follow him into a room. "But that's okay. I'll ask the registration clerk to come in to see you, to get everything rolling."

"Sorry," he murmured to Kylie. "I guess I didn't go through proper procedures by bringing you directly in."

Despite her obvious concern for Ben, she smiled. "You doctors are all the same, thinking you're above following the rules."

"Hey, I was hoping we wouldn't have to get charged an ED fee, that's all," Seth defended himself.

Kylie's smile faded. "We have insurance, so it's no problem. I'm sure this visit will be covered."

If not, he'd darn well pay it himself. But he didn't voice the thought as Maggie, the registration clerk, arrived. Maggie greeted him briefly, and then entered all the pertinent information from Kylie about Ben into her laptop computer.

"Will someone let us know when Dr. Greenley arrives?" Kylie asked, glancing at her watch. It had taken a while for the doctor to get back to her once she'd left the message with his answering service.

"I'm sure they will." Seth poked his head out of the room, noticing the ED wasn't too busy. There was only a handful of rooms with patients in them. Perhaps coming in during the middle of a Packers game was actually a good strategy. "I'll watch for him."

Kylie clung to Ben's hand, trying to put on a brave front although he could tell she was tense.

He pulled his gaze away, sweeping the ED area, and noticed a tall man in his midthirties talking to Simon. In a few minutes he headed in their direction.

Dr. Greenley? Having never met the man, he'd expected him to be older. He'd imagined a Santa Claus type of guy, a little rotund, with white hair and a beard. Not someone about his age, who seemed to appeal to the women—at least from what he could tell from a few of the nurses' reactions to him.

And, since he wasn't wearing a wedding ring, he had to assume Greenley wasn't married, either.

"Kylie? Ben?" Dr. Greenley barely spared Seth a glance as he came into the room, going directly to Ben's side. "So, your vision seems to be getting worse, hmm?" he asked, addressing Ben.

"Yeah, it's blurry," Ben said.

"Along with some double vision," Kylie added.

"We need to examine you again, young man." Dr. Greenley glanced around. "They have a special eye exam room here. I'll just go find out if it's open."

"I'll get it," Seth offered, knowing exactly where the eye exam room was. He should have taken Kylie and Ben there right away.

Seth stepped out into the area and immediately Alyssa, the charge nurse on duty, crossed over. "Hey, Seth, what do you need?"

"Would you unlock the eye exam room for us?" The charge nurse always carried the keys.

"Sure." He and Alyssa led the way, with Kylie, Ben and Dr. Greenley following close behind as they made their way through the ED to the exam room. Alyssa opened the door and stepped back. The eye exam room was small, barely large enough for all four of them to fit inside, but just when he'd considered stepping out, too, to give Kylie and Ben more room, Kylie slipped her hand into his, hanging on tight.

Dr. Greenley lifted Ben up into the chair and began using the complicated set of eye exam equipment to peer into Ben's eyes.

Surprised by the way she'd reached out for him, Seth drew Kylie closer and lowered his mouth to her ear. "Are you all right?"

"A little nervous," she confessed.

He gently squeezed her hand, wishing he could offer more than mere hand-holding for support. But he was pleased she'd accepted even that much from him. "It'll be all right. No matter what happens, I'll be here for you." He was a bit surprised at how much he meant it. But parenting was a tough job. He didn't like the idea of her dealing with Ben all alone.

Had that been partially why his own father had been so great with him and his siblings?

"I need to give you a couple of eye drops, Ben."

Seth glanced at Kylie, half expecting Ben to put up a fuss, but he had to hand it to Greenley—the guy had expertly put the drops in so fast Ben had barely noticed.

While they waited for the medication to work, he continued to hold Kylie's hand, gently rubbing her cold fingers. He'd already accepted the fact that their dinner plans were shot. Heck, even if Ben didn't get admitted to the hospital, which he seriously suspected might happen, Kylie wouldn't leave her son alone at a time like this.

He understood. Ben's eyesight was too important. Children tended to adapt better than adults did to having vision from only one eye, but that made Ben's right eye all the more important. And who knew what his future held? Maybe he'd have other vision problems, too, on top of this one. He was too young to start out with such a disadvantage.

"Hmm." Dr. Greenley made some annoying non-descript sounds as he examined Ben. Finally he turned toward Kylie. "I'm afraid Ben does have a detached retina. He'll need to be admitted to the hospital tonight. I'll need to do surgery on his left eye first thing in the morning."

"Surgery!" Kylie's hand tightened around his. "How dangerous is detached retina surgery?"

"Well, every surgical procedure has its risks. He'll need to be placed under general anesthesia, due to his young age. But I think I can repair the detached retina without too much trouble. I'd like to keep him in the hospital at least for a night or two afterwards, to keep him quiet and sedated."

Kylie glanced up at Seth, as if silently asking for his opinion. He nodded, agreeing with Greenley's assess-ment. "I think it's a good idea, Kylie. Ben is still growing. We don't know for sure if he'll become near-sighted or far-sighted as he grows. He's too young to suffer such a significant loss of vision."

"You're right. I know you are. It's just so hard to agree to such a drastic step as having surgery." Kylie bit down on her lower lip nervously. "But I don't want him to lose the vision in his left eye, either."

Dr. Greenley gently took her hand in his. "We have some excellent pediatric anesthesiologists on staff," he told her, giving her hand a squeeze. "He'll be in good hands."

"I know. Thanks for everything."

Greenley let her go, stood and made his way to the door. "I'll write the admission orders for Ben and see a nurse about assigning a room. I'll get someone from anesthesia to come and evaluate him as soon as you're settled."

"Okay." Kylie's eyes were a little dazed, as if she still hadn't realized the full impact because everything was happening so fast.

Seth took them back to the main area, trying to catch Alyssa's eye to speed up the admission process. The sooner he could get Kylie and Ben into a private room, the better.

He listened as Kylie explained to Ben about the surgery, how it wouldn't really hurt much at all, especially because he'd be asleep during the procedure. Ben took the news with a solemn braveness that made his throat close up.

Alyssa returned. "Okay, I have a room assignment for you. Ben will be on the third floor pediatric wing. There's a roll-out sofa bed for the parents, if you decide to stay overnight."

"Absolutely. I'm staying," Kylie said.

Seth had never doubted it. Alyssa processed the paperwork and then helped move Ben onto a gurney when the transporter arrived. Seth accompanied them upstairs, waiting patiently until Ben had been fully admitted before turning to Kylie.

"Do you want me to run back to your house to pack a suitcase for the two of you?" he offered.

"I could use a few personal items," Kylie admitted, running her hand through her hair. "But, actually, I'd really rather run home to get them myself. Would you mind staying here with Ben?"

Considering he probably wouldn't even know what to pack for a six-year-old, much less maintain his composure as he riffled through her underwear drawer, he quickly agreed.

"I wouldn't mind at all. Do you have your car keys?" he asked, remembering how he'd driven her car here to the hospital.

"I have them." She pulled the keys from her purse. Still she seemed to hesitate, as if worried about leaving her son even for a few minutes. "I won't be long," she promised, bending over to kiss Ben's cheek.

"It's okay. Me and Seth will be here." Ben had already found the remote for the television. "Hey, look, the Chicago Bears game is on."

"Figures," he said with a sigh, settling in on the chair next to Ben. "We missed most of the Packers game. But it looks like we won."

"So far the Bears are winning, too," Ben pointed out.

"Not for long," Seth joked. "They always choke in the last quarter."

"No, they don't," Ben protested loyally.

"Yes, they do," Seth insisted.

Kylie slipped from the room, the car keys jingling in her hand as she walked away. He gazed after her thoughtfully, impressed and humbled at how she'd entrusted him to look after her most cherished possession.

Her son.

CHAPTER EIGHT

KYLIE drove home to pack overnight bags for her and Ben. She also included her laptop computer so she could do some work while Ben was in surgery. She made it back to the hospital in record time, even though she knew full well Ben was in good hands with Seth.

After slinging her duffel bag over her shoulder, she picked up her computer case and strode into the hospital, taking the elevator up to Ben's room. She had to smile when she saw the two of them engrossed in the football game. Dr. Greenley had put a patch over Ben's injured eye, so he wouldn't strain it or get a headache from the double vision, but otherwise her son didn't look sick at all.

Eye surgery wasn't that big of a deal, she reminded herself. Complications from anesthesia were very rare. There was no reason to worry.

Although telling herself that and actually relaxing about the whole thing were two different issues.

Ben cheered when the Bears won their game. Seth grinned and confidently told Ben that it didn't matter if the Bears won or not, because when the two teams faced off in a few weeks the Packers were going to kick the Bears' butts.

Ben stubbornly refused to believe it.

The rivalry was all in good fun, and she could tell Ben relished the attention.

Seth stood as if preparing to leave just when Ben's second shift nurse, Celeste, walked in. "Hi, Seth. Er— what are you doing here?" Her curious gaze rested on Kylie and Ben.

"Hi, Celeste. Have you met Kylie Germaine, the new Cedar Bluff Paramedic Education Coordinator?"

"No, I haven't, but it's nice to meet you." Celeste flashed a warm smile, although Kylie suspected the nurse was already pairing her up with Seth as if they were a couple. She inwardly cringed at the rumor potential.

"Same here," she said, forcing a smile. "And this is my son, Ben." Kylie wanted to announce that she and Seth were just friends, but since it seemed awkward she kept her mouth shut.

"Dinner should be here shortly. Do you want a parent tray?" Celeste asked. "Don't worry about eating in front of Seth. He gets free food for the month as a result of winning the annual baseball game."

"A parent tray would be great." Kylie frowned at Seth. "I can't believe you get free food for a whole month just because you won a game."

Seth shrugged. "When you're good, you're good."

Kylie rolled her eyes and shook her head. No worries about his ego, obviously. Although she couldn't help glancing at the clock, wondering when he was planning to leave. Not that she didn't enjoy his company. But Seth clearly knew most of the hospital staff by name. This hospital's environment was close-knit, very similar to the community it served.

The longer he stayed with her, the more people would talk.

Finally he stood again, glancing down at her. "Kylie, are you going to be all right tonight?" Seth asked. "I can stay with you, if necessary."

Stay? As in share the single pull-out bed? Aghast, she quickly shook her head. "No, thanks, we'll be fine. Honestly." Then she frowned, realizing he didn't have a ride home. "Do you want me to take you back to pick up your car?"

"No, I can hitch a ride with someone, no problem." He frowned, as if he didn't want to leave her alone. "Are you sure you don't want me to stay?"

"Yes, I'm sure." Seth had already gone above and beyond normal friendship just by bringing her and Ben here. The last thing she needed was to continue to lean on him. She made sure her smile was confident. "Thanks anyway."

"I'll see you both in the morning, then." Seth hesitated by the doorway, as if he'd hoped she'd walk him out, but she stayed right where she was.

"Don't make a special trip in. We'll be fine."

He frowned. "I have to work anyway, so I'll check in before the start of my shift." He lifted a hand and then left.

Kylie sighed and closed her eyes, rubbing her temple. Ridiculous to feel alone just because Seth was gone. Hadn't she raised Ben on her own for the past six years? Why was she suddenly wishing for more?

Because of those stolen kisses, that was why. She was letting her loneliness get to her. Seth might be a great distraction for now, but she knew very well he wasn't a guy she could count on for the long term.

Okay, she needed something else to think about other than Seth. So, while Ben was engrossed in the Disney Channel, she pulled out her laptop and did some work. When she'd finished the first part of the new paramedic training program Ben was falling asleep, so she pulled out the roll-away bed and changed into a pair of comfy sweats. No way was she going to parade around the hospital in her pajamas.

Sleep didn't come easily. No matter how much she knew it was useless to worry, she couldn't help thinking about all the worst-case scenarios. What if Ben had a reaction to some medication? Or to the anesthesia? What if the surgery didn't work and he lost the vision in his left eye? She tossed and turned, sleeping in brief snatches of time but not really resting.

The next morning a nurse woke Ben early, because his eye surgery was scheduled as the first case. Kylie quickly showered and changed, even though it was barely five-thirty in the morning.

"Mom, I'm hungry. And thirsty." Ben was cross. The thrill of the Disney Channel and the novelty of being in the hospital weren't enough to keep him satisfied any longer.

"Ben, I'm sorry, but you can't have anything to eat or drink." His plaintive expression wrenched her heart. This was the hard part of parenting. If she could take over Ben's discomforts for him, she would. "After surgery is over, then you'll get something to drink."

"But I'm hungry and thirsty *now*."

Her son's querulous tone made her sigh helplessly. Luckily the nurse returned, pushing an OR cart.

"Hop over, Ben. We're going to take you on a ride down to the operating room."

Distracted, her son scrambled over to the cart, and Kylie crossed over to walk down with him. She was glad Ben didn't seem to be overly nervous about the event.

"The doctor is going to put you to sleep, so you won't feel a thing," the nurse explained as they made their way to the elevator. "When you wake up, you'll feel drowsy for a while, but once the anesthesia wears off you'll be fine."

Sure, unless there were complications. But Kylie refused to let her thoughts show. "And you'll get to eat and drink anything you want," she added.

"Okay." Ben glanced around at the nearly empty halls. "Can't you push me faster?" he asked, as if the cart were some sort of amusement ride.

"Nope, sorry. This is as fast as I go," the nurse answered with a laugh.

At the doorway to the operating room the nurse halted the gurney with an apologetic glance. "Sorry, Mom, but this is as far as you get to come along."

Kylie forced a smile, ignoring the knot in her stomach. Reaching over the side rail of the gurney, she gave Ben a big hug and a kiss. "See you in a couple of hours, Ben. I love you."

His arms tightened around her neck, as if he suddenly

realized having surgery might be a big deal. But the sedative the nurse had given him earlier helped keep him calm. "I love you too, Mom."

As the nurse wheeled him through the doors, she felt her eyes filling with tears. She brushed them aside and turned, running headfirst into Seth.

"Hey, are you all right?" He captured her shoulders in his hands before her nose smashed into his chest.

"Fine." She sniffled and gave a halfhearted smile. "I'm just overreacting a bit."

"I'm sorry I missed him," Seth said, not seeming to be in any hurry to let her go. His hands were warm and strong on her shoulders. "I tried to get here earlier, but there was a crash on the highway and traffic was backed up for miles."

"It's okay. He'll be fine." She longed to throw herself into his embrace, so she forced herself to take a step back. His thoughtfulness to come and see Ben off to surgery was touching, but completely unnecessary. Somehow she had to forget those sizzling kisses and put her son's needs first, before her own. "Guess you'd better get back down to the ED, since you're working today."

"Yeah." He fell into step beside her as they slowly made their way down the hall toward the elevators. "Did they tell you how long he'll be in surgery?"

"Not more than a couple of hours."

Seth nodded. "Great. I'll dash up to check on Ben when there's a lull in the patient load."

She wanted to protest that it wasn't necessary, but knew that Ben would be thrilled to see him. "All right," she agreed.

At the elevators they paused, and from the expression on Seth's face he had something on his mind, but his pager chose that moment to chirp.

He unclipped it from his waistband and read the display. "I have to go. There's a patient on the way in."

"From the crash?" she guessed.

"Yes." He took her hand, reached over and brushed a quick kiss across her lips. "See you in a little while," he murmured.

Her mouth tingling, she could only nod in shocked surprise as he took the stairs down to the first floor ED.

He had to stop doing that, she thought, irritably jamming her finger on the button to summon the elevator. He really, *really* had to stop doing that.

Seth was acting as if they were already a couple.

But they weren't.

Her fault, since she'd allowed him to kiss her. Twice. Make that three times if you counted this most recent one. But enough was enough. This emotional roller-coaster ride needed to stop, now.

Determined to forget about Seth for a while, she returned to Ben's room. She tried to work on the training program, but found herself surfing the Internet instead.

She typed the name of Air Force pilot Shane Andre into the search engine. Through a process of elimination she was able to find an article talking about Shane Andre being declared missing in action when his helicopter went down during a mission to rescue American hostages in Iran. For several weeks no one had been sure if Shane Andre was alive or dead. He'd eventually been pronounced dead five weeks after he'd gone missing, when his military ID tags were found.

She saved the information to show Seth. Maybe he'd like to see how his father was portrayed as a hero.

For a long time she stared at the grainy picture of Seth's father. Seeing Seth's father made her think about Ben's. What was Tristan doing? Did he ever think about them? Ever wonder how his child was doing?

For a millisecond she considered calling Tristan to let him know about Ben's surgery, but almost immediately decided against it. After all, Tristan had made it clear he didn't want to be a father. And it wasn't as if Ben was having major surgery over some debilitating illness. Eye surgery wasn't anything to take lightly, but it was certainly not life-threatening.

No, there was no reason to call him. Tristan had made his choices a long time ago. He'd never gotten in touch with her—not once in the past six years. The last thing she wanted to do was open Ben up to pain and disappointment.

But as she shut down her computer she couldn't help wondering if someday Ben would try to track down Tristan the same way she'd just researched information on Shane Andre.

Seth pushed thoughts of Ben and Kylie out of his mind as he listened to the paramedic's report.

"Twenty-eight-year-old pregnant female with blunt trauma to her abdomen during the car crash. She's estimated to be thirty weeks pregnant with vital signs stable."

Seth was concerned about the way Josie, the pregnant

woman, was moaning in pain. And for some reason the paramedic's laid-back attitude bothered him, too. He wasn't sure he trusted the guy's assessment. "She seems to be in a lot of pain. What exactly are her vitals?"

"Her pulse is tachy at 128, and her blood pressure is elevated to 180/104—but I'm sure those elevations are mostly the result of the emotional stress of being in a car crash."

Seth didn't agree. "Eve, get the OB/GYN attending down here, stat. Let's give her some fluid volume and get a full set of labs, including sending a urine sample for protein." He turned toward the paramedic, whose name tag identified him as Craig. "You might want to brush up on your OB physiology. Because elevated blood pressure is *never* normal in pregnancy—not even after trauma."

"Well, she can't be bleeding—not with a blood pressure that high," Craig said defensively.

"No, but she could have preeclampsia," Seth countered, trying not to lose his patience. He mentally added this to the list of educational needs for the paramedics as he turned toward his patient. "Get me a Doppler so I can listen to fetal heart tones."

Practically before he'd finished speaking the nurse had shoved a Doppler in his hand. That was what he liked about the ED. The nurses were always one step ahead of him. He wanted to give Josie something to calm her down, but he didn't want to do anything that might impact the fetus, either.

"Shh, it's okay, Josie," Eve said soothingly. "We're going to take good care of you and your baby. Try not to get upset. Right now you need to calm down and relax."

"Hi, Josie, my name is Dr. Taylor. I'm going to examine you and your baby, okay? Take a deep breath for me and hold it." Seth told her that more to relax her than anything else, and the diversionary tactic seemed to work. "Good. Now, let it out slowly."

Seth could feel some mild contractions as he gently palpated her round abdomen. For a moment he imagined what it might be like if Kylie was pregnant with his child. Would Ben mind a little brother or sister? Pushing the crazy thought away, he reached for the Doppler gel.

"This is going to be cold against your skin," he informed Josie, hoping the OB/GYN attending would get here soon. "But then we're going to listen for your baby's heartbeat."

Focusing on the baby rather than on her traumatic experience seemed to help calm Josie down. She watched him intently as he used the Doppler to move around the gel on her belly, until the distinct sound of the baby's heartbeat filled the room.

"She's okay? My baby is okay?" Josie asked.

Seth nodded, grinning. "Yes, it sounds like your baby is doing fine. Her heartbeat is fast but steady." His smile faded, though, as one of the nurses handed him a slip of paper containing her lab results, confirming his worst fears. "Josie, how have you been feeling lately?"

Her lower lip trembled a little. "Not very good. I've been having bad headaches and episodes of sudden nausea with vomiting. I was on my way to my routine doctor's appointment when the other car ran a red light, hitting me broadside."

Headaches weren't too uncommon, but the sudden onset of nausea and vomiting during her third trimester concerned him. "Eve, take her blood pressure at frequent intervals. Where in the heck is the OB?"

"I'm here," a soft feminine voice said from behind him. He turned around to see a petite, strikingly beautiful redheaded woman he'd never seen before. "My name is Kim Rayborn and I'm the OB Attending on call. What's the situation at hand?"

Seth quickly filled her in on Josie's presenting signs and symptoms. He knew most of the attending physicians by name, so assumed Kim was new to Cedar Bluff. They sometimes lost their doctors to the bigger cities, where the pay was often higher. "We were trying to rule out preeclampsia, but here are her latest lab values. She's spilling quite a bit of protein in her urine."

Kim gave them a quick glance and then turned toward the patient. "Josie, my name is Kim, and I'm the OB doctor on call. Who is your regular OB physician?"

"Dr. Eric Kampine. Why?" Josie's eyes were wide as she astutely realized something was going on. "What's wrong?"

"You're fine, and your baby is fine," Kim gently reassured her. "But I'm concerned you have some signs and symptoms of preeclampsia, also known as toxemia. It's not life-threatening to you or your baby at this point, but it is something we need to treat. I'm going to admit you upstairs to the OB unit, and I'd like to give your doctor a call to let him know what's going on." Kim smiled and took Josie's hand. Seth was impressed with her calm bedside manner. "I promise I'll stay with you until your doctor arrives, all right?"

Josie nodded, clutching Kim's hand.

"I'd like to get her connected to a continuous fetal monitor. Do you have one down here, or should I send someone up to get one?" Kim asked.

"We don't have them here. We always borrow from the OB/GYN unit upstairs," Seth told her.

"Okay, then, let's get her up there as quickly as possible."

Kim wouldn't get an argument from him. Seth was glad he could safely hand over Josie's care to someone better prepared to deal with it. He'd only delivered a couple of babies in his career and he preferred to keep it that way. Pregnant women and babies made him nervous.

More than nervous. He'd always intended to stay far away from that scene. Watching his brother and sister falling in love had only reinforced how vulnerable they were to getting hurt down the road. He'd decided not to go down that path himself.

So why had he momentarily imagined how radiant and beautiful Kylie would look carrying a child? *His* child?

Rotating his head from side to side, he tried to ease the tension that had knotted there. He was tired, that was all. He hadn't slept well the night before, thinking about Kylie and Ben, wishing she'd asked him to stay. Heck, as if that hadn't been bad enough, she'd even followed him into his dreams.

There wasn't time to visit Kylie and Ben now, though. There was documentation and further assessment to do before Josie could be transferred upstairs with Kim. And there were still several other less urgent patients he needed to see.

It wasn't until later, when the bedlam had died down a bit and he was heading upstairs to see Ben, that he realized he hadn't experienced that same flash of interest with Kim that he normally did when he met a beautiful and potentially available woman.

Like when he'd first met Kylie.

He frowned, trying to figure out what was different. Kim was pretty, with her cloud of red hair, and she was smart. But he hadn't felt one iota of male interest—at least nothing more than friendly admiration. He hadn't experienced the slightest urge to ask her out, or to investigate whether she was seeing anyone.

The realization caused a flare of panic. Because even in the past, when he'd gone out with women for brief periods of fun, he'd felt that spark of interest when meeting someone new. It was one of the reasons he always made his no-strings intent clear up front. He'd always assumed commitment wasn't a part of his genetic DNA makeup.

Now he found he was only interested in one woman.

Kylie.

CHAPTER NINE

PATIENTLY waiting to hear news from the OR about Ben wasn't easy for Kylie. It was impossible to sit quietly, reading or working, when she had no idea how her son was doing. And since going to the gym or for a run to burn off her excess energy wasn't possible, she paced the small floor of Ben's hospital room instead.

Finally Dr. Greenley came up to see her, dressed in his OR scrubs, face mask dangling around his neck. "Kylie? Ben's surgery is finished. He's in the post-anesthesia care area now. As soon as he wakes up a bit more, the nurses there will bring him back up here to his room."

"He's okay?" she asked, coming to a halt in front of him, twisting her hands nervously. "The surgery went well?"

"The surgery went fine," he assured her with a gentle smile. "He remained very stable throughout the procedure. Of course, we'll want him to rest his left eye for a few days, so we won't know how well his vision has returned for some time yet. But I'm very optimistic he'll make a full recovery."

Optimism was good, right? The tightness in her chest

eased as she returned a weary smile. "I'm so glad to hear that, Dr. Greenley."

A flash of awareness brightened his eyes. "Please, call me Geoff."

"All right—Geoff." Using his name didn't come naturally, since she tended to keep things professional, but she'd noticed most of the hospital staff called the doctors by name, as if they were all on friendly terms. She'd learned to call Seth by his first name, hadn't she? "I must admit keeping Ben quiet for the next few days is probably going to be my greatest challenge."

Geoff chuckled. "You could be right. I can tell Ben's activity level is high enough to keep you on your toes."

That was putting it mildly, although she honestly didn't mind. "Very true. Seriously, though, how quiet does he need to be? Can he watch movies and TV?"

"Absolutely. Just keep him from running around or playing any types of sports for a few days."

She stifled a sigh, knowing from experience it wouldn't be easy—especially once Ben was feeling better. "All right."

"I'd like to keep him in the hospital one more night," Geoff said. "But if all goes well you can take him home in the morning. I'll see him in my office after the third day, so we can take the patch off and test his vision."

She nodded, appreciating his cautious approach. "Sounds good."

He took one step toward the door, as if to leave, then hesitated and turned back. "Kylie, do you mind if I ask you a personal question?"

She mentally braced herself, assuming Geoff wanted

to know about Ben's father, as most people did. She forced a smile. "No, of course I don't mind."

"Are you seeing anyone? Like in a relationship?" His tone was low, hesitant, as if it wasn't easy for him to ask.

Surprised, she simply stared at him for a moment, even as Seth's image flickered in her mind. She understood how Geoff might assume she and Seth were a couple, the way they'd been together in the emergency room yesterday. But a few brief kisses didn't mean much to a guy like Seth.

Amazing how two attractive men had asked her out in the past two weeks. A part of her was honored, but, seeing as she'd never considered Ben's ophthalmologist as a potential date, she wasn't sure how to respond. "No, I'm not seeing anyone. But I've been very busy, between getting settled in our new home, my new job responsibilities and raising Ben." She lifted her shoulder in a slight shrug. "To be honest, I really don't have time to dedicate to a relationship."

"I see." His self-deprecating smile told her he understood her subtle message that she wasn't interested, at least not right now. "Once things settle down, and if you do find some time on your hands, give me a call, okay?"

"Sure," she agreed, feeling a tiny wave of relief that he'd taken her rejection so well. He was a good-looking guy, and certainly nice enough, but for some reason she couldn't imagine going out with him. "Thank you again, for everything."

"You're welcome." This time he didn't hesitate as he walked out of Ben's hospital room.

She let out a sigh and ran her fingers through her hair.

Was she crazy to let a guy like Geoff Greenley walk away? She'd decided she didn't need a man to make her happy, and she didn't. Yet they still asked her out. From the brief interactions she'd had with the ophthalmologist she'd guessed he wasn't a player, like Seth seemed to be. She'd bet Geoff hadn't done anything to earn the nickname Romeo.

Tristan had hurt her, but she was smart enough to know that all men weren't like her son's father.

Maybe she *would* give Geoff a call when she had some free time. She still had his card.

"Kylie?" Seth's husky voice caused her to glance up quickly.

Her pulse leaped when she saw him standing in the doorway. He looked uncertain, as if unsure of his welcome. Every nerve in her body tingled with awareness, and her stomach clenched with the realization that she hadn't felt any of this tension, this sexual awareness and excitement, around Geoff.

Only for Seth.

She tried to cover up her body's untimely physical reaction. "Hi. You just missed Dr. Greenley. Ben's surgery went fine."

"I saw him leave," Seth admitted as he ventured further into the room. "I—uh—didn't want to interrupt."

Interrupt? She felt her cheeks flush and hoped Seth hadn't overheard their conversation. At least not the part where Geoff had asked her out. How did she get into these situations, anyway? Time to change the subject. "Ben's in the recovery area now. He should be transferred up here soon."

"That's good. I'm glad the surgery went well." He wasn't smiling. His hands were tucked into the deep pockets of his lab coat and he wasn't meeting her gaze, at least not for more than a nanosecond. Why did she get the feeling he was trying to put some distance between them?

He was the one who'd kissed *her* this morning, not the other way around.

Seth didn't do relationships, she reminded herself. Things would be better all round if they simply remained good friends. "Oh, before I forget, I have something to show you." She crossed over to her laptop computer and turned it on, tapping her foot impatiently as it took a while to power up.

"Yeah?" His expression was perplexed as he came up to stand beside her.

"By the way, how's your patient?" she asked, desperate for something to talk about while the computer program took forever to download. "The one from the car crash?"

"She and her baby are hanging in there."

"Baby?" She gasped. "Good grief, your patient was pregnant?"

Seth nodded. "Yeah, but she was pretty lucky. Especially considering the paramedic crew didn't feel her high blood pressure was anything to worry about. She's okay from the crash, but is currently being treated in the OB unit for preeclampsia."

"Oh, dear. I hope she and the baby will both be all right." Finally the software program was running. "I'll add OB pathophysiology to my list of topics to cover during our next paramedic training session," she added as she clicked the buttons to bring up the Web page.

"Good idea," Seth replied. He glanced at the article she'd pulled up and frowned. "What's this?"

"An article about your biological father, Shane Andre." The dark furrow between his eyes made her wonder if she'd made a mistake to bring this bit of news to his attention. Helplessly, she waved a hand at the screen. "I just thought you'd be interested to know your father is considered a hero."

He didn't say anything right away, his gaze riveted on the laptop screen. After a few minutes he glanced at her. "Thanks, Kylie. It was nice of you to do this. But I don't know if it matters or not. The whole situation seems so surreal." He turned away, as if he didn't want to read any more.

"Seth, he didn't leave you and your siblings on purpose," she said softly. For some reason she wanted to help him come to grips with his past.

Seth let out a frustrated sigh. "I know you're right. But for some reason it still feels like a betrayal."

"A betrayal on your mother's part? Because she didn't tell you?" she asked.

He nodded, hunching his shoulders a bit. "I just wish I understood why she kept the secret, that's all."

Secrets were tough. Hadn't she felt the same betrayal when Tristan had announced he was leaving the moment she told him she was in labor? Talk about bad timing. And all those months she'd waited for him to change his mind hadn't been easy, either.

Because Tristan hadn't changed his mind.

"Just remember she loved you," she suggested.

Before Seth could respond, Ben was wheeled into the room on a stretcher. Her son looked so small and helpless lying there with a large eyepatch over his left eye, she couldn't help feeling a twinge of panic.

"Ben." She quickly crossed over to where the nurse was maneuvering the cart alongside the bed. She took Ben's hand in hers. "How is he?" she asked.

"A little nauseous, I'm afraid," the nurse said with a note of apology. "I've given him a dose of Compazine, so hopefully that should help."

"Mom?" Groggy from the anesthesia, Ben lifted his head. "I don't feel good. My tummy hurts."

"I'm sorry, sweetheart. The nurse gave you some medicine, so you should feel better soon."

The nurse put down the side rail of the cart. "Ben, do you think you can scoot over to the bed for me?"

"I'll lift him," Kylie said, stretching over the mattress of the bed to reach for her son. Seth came up beside her and with his longer arms lifted Ben and gently placed him in the center of the bed. "Thanks," she murmured.

Ben didn't seem to notice his idol Seth was there. Looking miserable, he curled into a ball, clutching his stomach. Hating to feel so helpless, Kylie bent over and pressed a soft kiss on the tender spot above his temple.

"The nausea should pass soon," Seth said.

"I hope so." She hated seeing Ben like this.

Seth pulled up a chair for her, so she could sit right next to Ben's bed. She silently thanked him with a warm look.

He pulled up a second chair for himself. She was surprised he didn't take the opportunity to slip away. She should have urged him to go, if only to help keep the rumors at bay, but she didn't.

Despite her determination to keep things friendly between them, she was too grateful for his quiet strength and support.

Seth swallowed a groan as he lifted his head. The muscles of his neck tightened painfully from the awkward way he'd fallen asleep in the chair.

It was early, he guessed, peering at the clock on the wall. Yep, barely five in the morning. It had been a long night. Ben's nausea hadn't gotten any better until they'd agreed to give him some stronger anti-nausea medicine called Zofran.

He stretched his neck side to side in an effort to loosen the muscles as his gaze sought and found Kylie, sleeping with her head cushioned on the mattress beside Ben. He hoped she'd slept better than he had. She hadn't asked him to leave, so he'd stayed—although the only thing he'd been any help with was suggesting the stronger anti-nausea medication for Ben.

He wished he could have done more.

Scrubbing a hand over the stubble on his cheek, he knew he should find a razor and a toothbrush. He was scheduled to work this morning, so he needed to be somewhat presentable. Thank heavens the hospital would supply another pair of scrubs for him to wear.

He eased out of the chair, trying to be quiet, but Kylie awoke, lifting her head. "Seth?"

Her husky voice saying his name sent a shaft of

desire straight to his groin. He battered down the sexual awareness and smiled. "How are you?"

"Okay, I guess." She yawned, and he itched to pull her soft, sleepy body against his. "Where are you going?" she whispered, so as not to wake Ben.

"I have to work." He tucked his hands into the pockets of his lab coat to keep from reaching for her. With her tousled hair and soft, rosy skin she was so beautiful it made his chest ache.

"Oh." Was that disappointment shimmering in her eyes? "You need your sleep. You shouldn't have stayed here all night if you had to work."

First she was disappointed that he had to leave, and now she was concerned about his welfare. Her caring was a novelty. His relationships in the past had always been about fun. Light and friendly fun. This felt like so much more.

Things were different with Kylie.

Or maybe he was just a different person with Kylie?

"I'll be fine," he assured her, trying to smile.

She bit her lower lip in that endearing habit she had. It made him want to kiss her.

Which only reminded him how Greenley had asked her out. He'd been standing outside the door, double-checking a recent page, and hadn't been able to help overhearing them talk. He should have walked away, but when he'd heard Greenley ask her if she was seeing anyone he'd held his breath, waiting for her answer.

No, I'm not seeing anyone. I really don't have time for a relationship.

Her words had cut deep. They shouldn't have bothered him, but they did. *He* was the one who'd always kept his distance from women. *He* was the one who'd created the no-strings rule.

A rule he suddenly wanted to toss out the window.

Ironic that he'd been running from relationships for years, only to want one now with a woman who didn't appear to feel the same way.

"Thanks for staying, Seth," she was saying now, still in a quiet voice so as not to disturb Ben. "Dr. Greenley plans on discharging Ben today, so I'll probably take him home before you get off work. Ben won't be allowed to have the eyepatch off until our appointment on Thursday."

"I see." His stomach felt as if it were being twisted by a meat grinder. So this was it, then? After the closeness they'd shared over the past few days, this was it? He wouldn't see her again until she was back at work, transporting patients in from the field?

No way. Absolutely not.

This must be how women had felt when he'd left them. Especially Rachel, the baseball pitcher. Maybe he'd been unfair all these years. Maybe his aversion to relationships was only because he hadn't given them a fair chance?

"What about our dinner?" he asked, trying not to sound desperate. "I'd like to cash in on my rain check once Ben is feeling better."

Her hesitation didn't help his ego any. After what seemed like an hour, but was probably only a few minutes, she nodded. "Sure. We could do that."

He willed his tense muscles to relax. "I'll call you,

okay? Besides, I'd like to check up on Ben—to see how he's doing."

"All right." He was glad when she smiled.

"Take care, Kylie." He wanted to pull her into his arms for a kiss, but figured that might be pushing it, considering Ben was sleeping right there. It would be just his luck the boy would wake up at the wrong moment.

"Bye, Seth." She didn't move toward him, but stayed right beside Ben, so he forced himself to leave.

But walking away from Kylie and Ben was far more difficult than he'd ever imagined.

The ED was busy over the next few days, but Seth didn't forget about Kylie or Ben. In fact he hated the thought of Kylie going to see Greenley on Thursday. What if the guy asked her out again and this time she decided to go? Maybe she'd think Greenley was a better risk for a relationship than he was? The possibility haunted him, so he called her the night before the follow-up appointment.

"Hi, Seth." He hoped he wasn't imagining the warmth in her voice. "Ben has been asking about you."

"He has?" The knowledge that Ben had missed him brought a surge of tenderness to his heart. Although he'd rather know that Kylie had missed him. "I'm off work tomorrow. Would you like company for Ben's doctor's appointment?"

"No. I'm sure you have other things to do with your day off," Kylie chided. "However, if things do go well tomorrow, I was thinking of booking a babysitter for Friday night."

Friday night? His heart leaped with anticipation.

But wait, he was supposed to work Friday night. Thankfully there were a few people who owed him a favor. He'd never maneuvered a night off before. Hadn't ever found a woman important enough to work around his hectic schedule.

"Unless you've changed your mind about dinner," Kylie said, misinterpreting his silence.

"Not a chance," he assured her. "I'd love to take you to dinner Friday. I was supposed to work, but I'm pretty sure I can switch with someone."

"Oh, I should have thought to ask," Kylie said. "If you can't find someone to switch we'll go another day. It's not a big deal."

He vehemently disagreed. Dinner with Kylie was a very big deal. Since he was supposed to work Saturday, too, he didn't suggest a different night. "It should be no problem. I'll call you tomorrow, just to confirm."

"Sounds good." There was a pause before she asked, "Ben wants to say hi."

"Sure. Put him on." There was a brief silence as the phone switched hands.

"Dr. Seth? How are you?"

Ben's childish voice caused a lump to form in the back of his throat. "I'm great, but the better question is how are *you*? No more feeling sick to your stomach, I hope?"

"Nope. I'm all better. Except Mom won't let me play outside with my friends."

He lifted a brow at the querulous note in Ben's voice. Poor Kylie had really had her hands full in trying to get Ben to rest. He found himself wanting to help in any way he could. "Ben, your mother is following the doctor's orders. You're not supposed to play outside with your friends. Not until we know your eye is fully recovered."

"It doesn't hurt, so it must already be fully recovered."

"Pain isn't the only thing to worry about. Remember when you had blurry vision?"

"Yeah," Ben agreed reluctantly.

"Give your mom a break. If you behave yourself and listen to your mom, I'll take you to the Packers-Bears game in Chicago next weekend."

"Really?" Ben's enthusiasm radiated through the phone line. "That would be so cool!"

Now that he thought about it, he realized he should have talked to Kylie about it first. "Ah, you'd better let me ask your mom about it, okay? I don't know how she's going to feel about going to a football game."

"She'll love it," Ben said confidently. "Football is awesome. Here's my mom. Bye, Dr. Seth."

When Kylie came back on the line, he tried to think of an easy way to broach the subject. She was smart enough to figure out he'd overstepped his bounds, though.

"Seth, what did you just bribe Ben with?" she asked in an exasperated tone. "He's promising to be good, but at the same time he's hopping around like a jumping bean."

"Kylie, don't be upset. It just so happens I have tickets to the Packers-Bears game in Chicago next weekend. I thought it would be fun if the three of us went together."

There was a long pause. "Seth, it's not that I'm against attending a football game, but Chicago is a pretty long drive. I don't think it's a good idea. Especially considering Ben starts his first day of school the very next day."

Well, that did complicate things. But the first day of school was fun, not exactly chock-full of hard work. "I was thinking we'd take the train down Saturday night. We could book a couple of hotel rooms so we don't have trouble with traffic. After the game we can simply take the train back home. We won't be out late, I promise."

"Obviously you have everything planned out." Her tart tone indicated she wasn't too happy about it, either.

"Kylie, I'm sorry. I should have spoken to you first. But do me a favor—don't decide anything right away. Think about it for a while. I know you're not a huge football fan, but seeing the game in person, feeling the excitement of the crowd—it's amazingly different when you're sitting in the stands compared to watching it on television."

"I'll think about it," she said slowly. "But no more promises to Ben without talking to me first."

"Agreed." He was glad she wasn't too mad. "What time did you say your appointment was tomorrow?"

"Ten in the morning. But there's no reason to come with us. I'm sure everything will be fine."

"I don't mind. I'll be there to pick you and Ben up at nine forty-five. See you then." He quickly hung up before she could argue.

Because there was no way in hell he was letting her go see Greenley without him.

CHAPTER TEN

KYLIE hadn't really thought Seth would bother to drive over just to accompany them to Ben's doctor's appointment, but he did.

"I'll drive," she told him, when he sauntered up the driveway. Her dependable car sat in front of the garage, ready to go.

He didn't try to argue, especially since there was no way Ben's child safety seat would fit in his cherry-red Corvette. The car obviously wasn't built for a family, considering Charlene didn't even have a backseat. Just seeing him with his racy car only reinforced how wrong they were together.

No matter how much she liked him.

"So, Ben, how are you?" Seth asked, as she clicked on her seat belt and started the car.

"Good. Although I can't play outside until this patch comes off."

She had to suppress a grin. Playing outside at day care was Ben's favorite part of the day.

"Have you been listening to your mom, like I told you?" Seth asked in a stern voice.

Ben nodded enthusiastically. "Yep. And I told all the kids at day care how we were going to the Packers versus Bears game."

She tried not to think too much about the football game. She still wasn't convinced it was a good idea to go. Especially right before the first day of school. Not that the kids would do much on the first day. But heck, she didn't even *like* sports much.

Although the baseball game hadn't been too bad. Not that she remembered much, except Seth's home run and the heated kiss they'd shared.

Which wasn't going to happen again, she reminded herself sternly.

The ride to Dr. Geoff Greenley's office wasn't far. Kylie wished Seth would wait in the car. It felt awkward to walk in with him, especially after she'd told Geoff she wasn't seeing anyone.

"Hi, Kylie, Ben." Geoff greeted them cheerfully, although his gaze narrowed on Seth.

"Dr. Greenley—er—Geoff, this is Seth Taylor, a friend of ours." Kylie made the introductions, somewhat annoyed at the way the two men eyed each other warily. For heaven's sake, they looked as if they were ready to fight to see who would win the prize. She didn't appreciate their male posturing one little bit. "Seth, you remember Geoff Greenley from Ben's visit to the emergency department, don't you?"

"Sure." To give him credit, Seth stepped forward and offered his hand. "Nice to see you."

"Likewise." Geoff sounded anything but happy as he

reluctantly returned the greeting. He brightened for Ben. "Are you ready to lose that eyepatch?"

"Yeah." Ben reached up to finger the gauze, his tiny forehead puckering in a frown. "Will it hurt?"

"No, it won't hurt at all." Geoff patted the chair surrounded by the eye examination equipment. "Hop up here and I'll take it off for you."

Seth stood next to Kylie, toward the back of the exam room, his arms crossed over his chest. She flashed him an exasperated look, which he studiously ignored. What was wrong with him? Seth was acting like he'd come along for the sole purpose of staking his claim in front of Geoff.

Irritated, she focused on Ben, who was shielding his left eye against the bright light. If Seth thought she was impressed by his me-Tarzan, you-Jane imitation he was very much mistaken.

"Just give it a few minutes," Geoff advised as he used his ophthalmoscope to peer into Ben's eye. "Your vision will be blurry at first, but it should get better as we go along."

And what if it didn't get better? She had to bite down on her lip so she wouldn't interrupt Geoff as he was asking Ben a whole series of questions.

"Tell me—is this better, or this one?" Geoff flipped lenses in front of Ben's eyes as he proceeded through the examination.

Kylie was aware of Seth standing beside her. Although the inches between them felt more like miles. Maybe her agreeing to dinner was a mistake. She didn't have to go. It wasn't too late to cancel the babysitter. Although if she made a habit of canceling, Elise might not give her a third chance. Good babysitters were hard to find.

Back and forth, thoughts bounced through her mind like ping-pong balls. Should she? Or shouldn't she go? Was this a mistake? Or could it possibly be the beginning of something special? She had no idea what to do, and tried to focus her attention on Ben's answers to Geoff's questions.

"His vision is great," Geoff proclaimed, sitting back and grinning at Ben. "Both eyes have the same clarity of vision. He's all healed."

"That's wonderful news," she said, stepping forward to give Geoff a grateful smile. "Thanks so much for your help."

Seth, who hadn't uttered a sound since she'd introduced them, chose that minute to speak up. "By the way, Kylie, everything is set for Friday night. We have dinner reservations at seven."

She stared at him, barely resisting the urge to kick him in the shins to shut him up. Why had he blurted *that* out? Without bothering to respond to his ridiculous statement, which had absolutely no bearing on the conversation at hand, she turned back to Geoff, who watched them warily. "Do you need to see Ben again, for any more follow-up visits?"

"Not anytime soon, unless something changes. I'd like to see him again in six months, though." Geoff's expression seemed a little hurt when he met her gaze, and she wanted to explain that her being here with Seth wasn't what he thought.

Except it was.

Her stomach clenched with the realization. She could deny it all she wanted, but having dinner with Seth *was* a date. Worse, she *wanted* it to be a date.

Kissing him had made her long for more.

After thanking Geoff again, she hustled Ben out to the car. Seth walked beside her, seemingly oblivious to her pique.

"You didn't have to do that," she said half under her breath, mad enough to risk Ben overhearing.

"Do what?" Seth feigned innocence.

Suddenly she understood exactly what had happened to make Seth act like an idiot. "You overheard us talking that day in Ben's room, didn't you?" she accused.

Seth opened the back passenger door and gestured to the child safety seat. "In you go, Ben." While she watched, he took the time to make sure her son was securely strapped in.

When he closed the car door, she grabbed his arm. "Didn't you?" she asked again.

"You'd have to be blind not to see how he wants to be far more than Ben's eye doctor. He wants to go out with you, Kylie. I needed to tell him to back off."

"*You* needed to tell him? Why? You don't have any claim on me, Seth." For all her protests, she couldn't ignore the warmth creeping through her insides at his fierce protectiveness. The idea of two men wanting her was an anomaly. But all she really cared about was Seth.

"Oh, really? Did something change? Are you interested in seeing him on a personal level?" Seth asked in a dangerously low voice.

She swallowed hard at the fierce intensity in his eyes, but couldn't lie. "No."

He stared down at her for a long minute. The tension sizzling between them was so thick she thought it might choke her. But then he simply asked, "Do you want to drive?"

"Yes." She let out her breath in a huff. Annoyed with him—with all men—she stomped around to the driver's seat.

They didn't talk the entire ride back to her house. She parked in the driveway, avoiding his gaze. They all got out of the car, and once Ben had dashed into the house Seth turned to her.

"I'll pick you up tomorrow at six-thirty."

This was her chance to tell him to forget it, to explain how she'd changed her mind about going out to dinner— but her mouth didn't follow her brain's command.

"Fine," she heard herself say. "I'll see you to-morrow." She spun away, following Ben inside before she broke down and invited Seth in.

But she couldn't help watching through her front window as Seth climbed into his car, revving Charlene's engine a bit before driving away.

She closed her eyes and shook her head. Men. God must have put them on the planet solely to drive women crazy. This was exactly why she'd avoided them for the past few years.

So why couldn't she imagine going out with any other man? A guy like Geoff?

And, worse, why was she so looking forward to seeing Seth again Friday night?

* * *

Seth stared blankly at the ceiling above his head, although it was too dark to see anything clearly.

He was wired. Tense. Couldn't relax enough to fall asleep, no matter how many deep breathing exercises he did.

It was all Kylie's fault.

He hadn't wanted to leave her house after Ben's doctor's appointment, but considering she hadn't invited him in he hadn't had too much of a choice.

Besides, he'd sensed she was still irked with him.

Hopefully she'd get over it. Seeing the expression of adoration on Greenley's face the moment Kylie had walked in, he'd figured his timing had been perfect. At least now the guy knew she was seeing someone.

Maybe he'd avoided relationships in the past, but not anymore. Not now. Whether Kylie realized it or not, she was involved with him. A fact he intended to bring to her attention tomorrow night at dinner. No more of these meetings with Greenley. He wanted Kylie to admit she was involved with *him*, Seth Taylor, and no one else.

At midnight, he gave up and climbed out of bed. Wearing only his boxers, he padded to the living room and flicked on a single lamp before throwing himself onto the sofa.

Now what? He wasn't in the mood to watch mindless television. Wasn't sure he could lose himself in a murder mystery, either.

He wanted Kylie.

His body tightened painfully as he remembered their kisses. The way her curves had felt pressed against him.

He stifled a groan. Don't go there, he warned himself. Thinking about Kylie and their physical attraction wasn't going to help him relax—not in the least.

He let out a heavy sigh, his gaze landing on the box of family photos he'd split into three piles, for himself, Tess and Caleb.

Drawn to the box, he sat up and pulled it closer. He lifted the photos out, placing them carefully off to the side, until he reached the bottom layer. The place where he'd found the information on his mother's first marriage to his biological father, Shane Andre.

The letters were still there, beckoning him. Reluctantly, yet unable to stop himself, he pulled them out. The paper was fragile, so he opened them with care, placing them in order. He figured if he was going to read his parents' private letters he should start at the very beginning.

The first one was dated a few months after their wedding, according to the date on the wedding photograph. His father wore a blue dress uniform, which told Seth he must have been in the service when they'd married.

Dear Shane

I miss you so much! It seems like forever instead of just ten weeks since our glorious honeymoon on Sanibel Island.

My love, I have something to tell you. I wish we could talk in person, but I can't wait any longer to share this news. I'm pregnant! We're going to have a baby. Our baby. I hope you're as thrilled as I am.

Please write me back as soon as you can. I

*hope you get your leave in the next four months,
as they promised. I'd love for you to feel your son
or daughter growing in my womb.*

*Stay safe, my love. Remember you have a
family now to come home to.*
I love you so much!
Your wife, Jan.

The letter made his eyes burn. He could only imagine
how difficult it must have been for his mother to be at
home while his father was far away on active duty. The
following letter was from his father.

My dearest Jan
*I'm proud and thrilled to know you're carrying
our child! You couldn't have given me a greater
gift of love. I will get the four day leave I was
promised in a few months, so we'll make plans to
meet soon. I can't wait to see your belly round
with the promise of our future.*

*Please don't worry about me. I love flying, and
I'm safe high above the action. I miss you very much,
but I'm also proud to know I'm serving our country.*

*Write to me often and tell me everything about
how you're feeling. I want to know everything the
doctor is telling you, too.*
Love, Shane.

Seth stared at the words his biological father had written
over thirty years ago. Who *was* this man who'd stolen his
mother's heart? It was interesting to realize he must get his

love of speed from his dad. When he was younger he'd even once toyed with the idea of being a pilot.

All the letters seemed to carry the same theme, of love and longing. Missing each other and living for the few days they'd get to share together every few months. The last one was from his mother, right after he himself had been born.

Dear Shane

We have another son! Seth Patrick Andre was born at three-fifteen in the morning, the biggest baby yet, at nine pounds and two ounces. He's so long—over twenty-two inches. I think he's going to be tall, like his daddy.

I wish you were here to see him. He's so beautiful. Caleb and Tess are too young to appreciate the newest addition to the family. Having three children is going to keep me insanely busy, but I still miss you.

Please come home again soon. Your children barely remember you, although I show them your picture every night so they can mention you in their prayers.

Please come home, Shane. Your new son wants to meet his father.

Your loving wife, Jan.

Seth stared at the last letter for a long moment. So that was it. His father had never gotten a chance to respond. The fact that his mother had actually had his father's letters meant he'd kept them safe, and that they'd been returned to her along with his other personal effects after his death.

Even Caleb and Tess hadn't really known their biological father. Clearly his mother had tried to bridge the gap with little success. His mother must have thought that since they didn't remember their father there was no sense in talking about him. Especially after she'd remarried.

The last bit of his resentment faded. Kylie was right. His mother had loved them. No doubt she'd done what she'd thought was best for them.

He put the letters away. Gregory Taylor had been a great father. When he'd died, Seth, Caleb and Tess had missed him terribly. Looking back, he could understand how that probably hadn't been the time for their mother to tell them the truth about their real father. The man they'd spent so very little time with over the short years of their parents' marriage.

The man who'd never even seen his third child.

Kylie dressed with care for her dinner with Seth, choosing a long-sleeved amethyst V-necked sweater dress that clung to her curves, hoping the cashmere blend would keep her warm in the cool September evening.

The fact that the fabric accented her curves only helped to give her some badly needed self-confidence.

She couldn't help staring at her reflection in the mirror, wondering why Seth was attracted to her. She wasn't beautiful by anyone's standards. Her mouth was too wide, her nose a little too big. He could have any woman he wanted—had in fact dated many of the pretty doctors and nurses at Cedar Bluff Hospital.

So why her? Why now?

She didn't have any answers. In fact, the more she thought about it the more she grew convinced that this intense attraction they shared couldn't possibly last. Not for the duration needed for a true relationship. What she felt when Seth touched her was probably similar to the heat and flash of a comet that quickly burned out.

She bit her lip, trying to quell a sense of panic. Was it the worst thing in the world if it didn't last? As long as Ben wasn't hurt, what difference did it make? She hadn't felt this longing for a man in a very long time. Maybe she owed it to herself to try and trust again? To trust Seth.

Putting a hand over her jumping stomach, she took a deep breath. She must be crazy to even contemplate such a drastic step.

The doorbell rang at precisely six-thirty, causing her pulse to spike with anticipation. Swallowing hard, she left her bedroom, closing the door behind her. Down the hall, she could hear Ben and Elise, the young babysitter, talking to Seth.

When she stepped into the living room, Seth's gaze cut to hers. The frank approval in his eyes as he stared at her made her feel special. Sexy. Desirable in a way she hadn't felt in years.

"You look beautiful, Kylie. Are you ready to go?"

For a crazy moment she knew she'd never be ready. Not for Seth. Not for the way he made her feel. But the knowledge didn't stop her from responding.

"Yes. I'm ready."

CHAPTER ELEVEN

KYLIE tried to relax as much as she could, considering she was seated next to Seth in his plush sports car. The interior of the vehicle exuded his sexy, masculine scent, making her feel light-headed. And she was hyperaware of him—from the way his strong hands held the steering wheel and shifted the gearstick, to the way his broad shoulders brushed ever so slightly against her.

After weeks of chatting with him about football, her son's accident and hypothermia protocols, she suddenly couldn't think of a single thing to say.

"I made reservations at the Blue Diamond Resort, overlooking Lake Michigan," he told her. "I hope you don't mind."

Since she'd never even heard of the place, it was difficult to mind. Her exposure to restaurants centered around child-friendly places. Haute cuisine wasn't something she indulged in on a regular basis.

She offered a weak smile. "Sounds good."

"Seems Ben is doing much better without the eye patch," he commented.

"Yes, he is. Although I don't think he'll be happy

until he gets that cast off his arm." Ben might be a safe topic of discussion, but Kylie couldn't imagine Seth had ever talked about kids during any of his other dates.

"Kylie, relax," he murmured, far too clued in to her discomfort. "You're supposed to be having fun tonight."

Fun. Okay, sure. She could do fun.

"I guess I am nervous," she admitted, feeling a desperate need to break the silence. "I haven't gone out with a guy in a really long time."

He swiveled his head to stare at her, before letting out a rueful laugh. "Which only means I'm one lucky son of a gun, doesn't it?"

She wasn't so sure, but didn't answer as he pulled into the parking lot of a large building built right on the edge of the rocky lakeshore. Tiny lights were sprinkled in a random pattern on the roof of the building, the effect not Christmassy but reminding her instead of stars twinkling in the sky.

Seth took her hand to help her out of the car, and didn't let go as they walked inside. The place was all black and chrome, with tall green plants and lots of glass windows. The minute he gave his name, the maître d' whisked them to a small, private corner table overlooking the lake, giving her a sense of being totally isolated from the rest of the diners.

The seats were positioned side by side on the corner of the table, rather than directly across from each other. And it seemed as if Seth touched her constantly. The intimacy of their surroundings along with his heated glances warned her he might have seduction on his mind.

An idea that both scared her to death and thrilled her at the same time.

"What would you like to drink?" he asked.

Since drinking around a man you were head-over-heels attracted to was hardly smart, she figured she would stick with water for the moment. "I'm fine right now, thanks. Although a glass of wine with dinner might be nice."

"I'll bring a wine list," the waiter said before he hurried off.

There were no prices on the menu, a fact that made her gulp nervously, but Seth didn't seem to care as they placed their order. No wonder she'd never heard of the restaurant. Any place that didn't list their prices on the menu was more than her pocketbook could handle.

Just more proof that Seth was out of her league.

Her mouth went dry as he took her hand. But he surprised her with his topic of conversation. "I read my mother's letters to my biological father last night."

"You did?" She was stunned he'd confided in her.

He nodded. "You were right. The letters showed my mother loved Shane Andre, but at the same time I could tell by reading them how much she missed him and hated being forced to live apart from him. And the last letter she sent was about me, and how much she wanted him to come home to meet his new son."

"Oh, Seth." She squeezed his hand, hurting for him. "I'm sorry. That must have been hard."

"Well, to be honest I suspected as much, considering he died just a few weeks after I was born. And besides, from what I read he hadn't been home much to see my brother Caleb or my sister Tess, either."

How difficult for his mother. From the article she'd found on the internet, Shane Andre had been missing in action for several weeks, too. Weeks in which Seth's mother hadn't known if Shane was alive or dead.

"Are you all right?" she asked softly.

He smiled. "Yeah. I think so. Anyway, I just thought you should know you were right. Reading the letters— well, they gave me some insight into my mother's decision. I think in her mind Gregory Taylor really did become our dad. Far more than Shane Andre had been. I'm at peace with what she did."

"I'm glad."

"So what about you?" he asked, sliding his thumb over the back of her hand in a caress she felt all the way up her arm. "I'm curious to know everything about you."

"Everything?" She couldn't imagine why he'd be interested.

"Maybe not everything. How about if you start with what brought you to Cedar Bluff?"

"Well, I could say it was the warm and friendly atmosphere of the town, especially one with such a fantastic view." She gestured to the window, displaying the white-tipped waves lapping rhythmically over the rocky shore. "But if you want to know the truth, my reasons for moving here were more pragmatic than that. I needed the job."

"Pragmatic?" He looked confused. "Aren't paramedics in high demand everywhere?"

She lifted her shoulder in a tiny shrug. "Sure, but not paramedic education coordinator positions. As a single mother, I really needed higher pay with less variable hours. But, even more, I needed to get out of the big city." The memory of the close call she and Ben had faced made her shiver. She'd gone the past week without having the nightmare once—a new record. She forced a smile. "Cedar Bluff was an answer to my prayers."

Seth didn't smile, and his fingers tightened on hers. "Kylie, what happened in Chicago?"

His observation skills were too sharp. She hadn't told anyone about what had happened in Chicago, mostly because there hadn't been anyone to tell. She was an only child, and her parents had been gone for a long time—the year after she'd graduated from high school, in fact. "There was a lot of crime in our area," she said, striving to keep her tone matter-of-fact. "I really didn't like exposing Ben to that environment."

He stared at her for a long moment, before slowly shaking his head. "That may be, but something else happened. Something that scared you."

Was she that transparent? She took a sip of water, swallowing hard. "Drug busts and robberies were fairly commonplace in our neighborhood. I wanted to move, was saving a portion of each paycheck, but it seemed like things kept going wrong, putting me back financially. One night a man broke into our apartment."

She hesitated, not wanting to remember how scared she'd been. The clichéd saying about your life passing before your eyes when you faced death was true. Very true. "He had a knife. I—I think he was on drugs of some sort. I heard him stumbling around in the kitchen and dialed 911 on my cell phone, but then I had to make sure Ben was safe."

"Oh, man," Seth whispered, momentarily closing his eyes. "Tell me you didn't leave your bedroom."

"I had to make sure Ben was safe," she repeated. What happened that night was forever etched in her mind. "I came out of my bedroom—just as he stepped into the hallway. I had a fist full of money—to help appease him, I guess—so I threw it at him, hoping he'd take the time to pick it up so I could slip into Ben's room. But he didn't. Instead he laughed and came directly toward me."

"Dear God." Seth's hand surrounded hers so tightly she nearly winced with pain. "Did he touch you? Hurt you?"

"I was lucky. The cut in my flank was small, only needed a few stitches. And the police arrived before he could carry out his intent to really hurt me."

"Thank God." Seth's reverent whisper echoed her own sentiment. For a long moment neither of them spoke. Then Seth brushed a soft kiss along the back of her knuckles.

"So now you know why trust is a bit difficult for me," she confided.

His gaze held hers. "Kylie, have I told you how glad I am that you chose to move to Cedar Bluff?"

His teasing tone made her smile, helping to put her dark past to rest. The intruder hadn't hurt her—not really. She knew from her ambulance runs that the outcome could have been much worse. "No, I don't think you have."

"Well, I *am* glad. Very glad."

As their dinner was served, Seth eased the discussion to lighter subjects. The food was scrumptious and the wine heady.

When they'd finished eating, she sat back with a contented sigh. "Delicious. The best meal I've ever tasted. Thank you, Seth."

"The pleasure was all mine," he said in a husky tone.

She didn't see how that was possible, but somehow in the magic of the evening she found herself struggling to believe. Maybe it was a little selfish to take this time away from Ben for herself, but she'd enjoyed Seth's company far more than she'd expected.

"Would you be willing to go back to my condo for another glass of wine?"

His condo? For wine? Or for something more?

His efforts at seduction were back in full force.

Seth held his breath, waiting for Kylie's response. As much as he wanted her to say yes, he was mentally preparing himself for her refusal.

Kylie had been through some difficult times in her life—more so than he'd realized. She'd need time before she'd be comfortable taking their relationship further. He understood, knowing she had Ben to think about. She was no doubt anxious to go home to check on her son.

"I'd like that," she said, so softly he thought he must have misunderstood.

"Really?" His hopeful response popped out of his mouth before he could stop it. *Smooth. Real smooth, Taylor,* he thought wryly. He pushed his chair back and stood. "Great."

He placed his hand in the small of her back as they weaved between a few tables through the restaurant toward the door. He couldn't conceive a coherent thought as they walked the short distance to his car.

"Do you know what I love best about Cedar Bluff?" Kylie asked, as he headed toward the highway.

"Besides me?" he asked.

She laughed, as he'd hoped she would. "I like the people. And, yes, that includes you. It's so amazing to me how friendly everyone is. One day, about a week and a half ago, I was at the grocery store when a woman came running over, profusely thanking me for taking care of her husband, Chuck. Her name was Estelle, and her husband had forgotten to take his insulin, so he'd had mental status changes from having high blood sugar. I have no idea how she remembered I was the paramedic who'd responded to the scene."

"We're a small community. The whole town probably knows you by now—at least by name."

"Maybe, but still it's nice to know people appreciate the help. Very different from Chicago, I must say."

"I bet." Many of the citizens of Cedar Bluff came in on a regular basis, when chronic health issues acted up. "I still get Christmas cards every year, delivered to the ED from some of my former patients' families."

"Wow. I don't think that ever happens in Chicago. Or if it does, not very often."

He reached over to take her hand. "Like I said, I'm very glad you chose to move here."

"Me, too." She didn't pull her hand from his grasp, so he gently rubbed his thumb along the back of her hand.

Her skin was like silk. It made his mouth go dry to

imagine her skin was just as soft everywhere else. All evening her subtle citrus scent had wreaked havoc with his concentration.

And now she was coming home with him, at least for a drink, maybe for a stolen kiss or two. He was glad he'd had the foresight to clean up his condo and buy wine. He didn't have to be embarrassed to bring Kylie into his home.

He parked in the underground garage and followed behind her as they climbed the steps to his condo. Strange, but as he led her inside and looked at the place through Kylie's eyes he didn't see a home.

Not like the home she shared with Ben.

Not like the home he and his siblings had grown up in.

For a moment he found himself wondering if he could be a surrogate father to Ben, the same way Gregory Taylor had been to him.

"Do you have pictures of your family?" she asked, moving through the modern open kitchen into the living room.

"Yes, on the end table there's a picture of my parents, and another one of me, Caleb and Tess on the day I graduated from medical school." He pulled two wineglasses out of the cupboard and opened the bottle of wine he'd bought earlier that day. After filling the glasses halfway, he carried them into the living room.

She was sitting on the sofa, looking at the picture of his parents. "Your mother was beautiful. It's easy to see the family resemblance between you three kids and your mom."

"Yeah." He handed her a wineglass and took the seat

right next to her. "In hindsight, I guess we should have realized there wasn't much resemblance to our father, though."

"Maybe not physically, but I think there's more to being a father than passing along your genes."

As much as he loved his family, he didn't really want to talk about them now. He watched as she took a sip of her wine, before placing the glass on the coffee table.

He set his glass beside hers, realizing he wanted to change the subject to something more important. Like the two of them. "Kylie, you were right. I did overhear the conversation you had with Greenley that day in Ben's hospital room."

She nodded, tilting her head to look at him thoughtfully. "I figured as much."

He pierced her with his gaze. "I didn't like it when you told him you weren't seeing anyone."

She raised a brow. "But we aren't seeing each other."

"What do you call this?" he asked, lightly stroking her shoulder.

"Ah—friends?" She tore her gaze from his, picked up her wineglass and then put it down without taking a sip.

Her nervousness made him think he was on the right track. "Are you telling me you don't feel a thing when I touch you like this?" He slid his hand along the side of her neck, cupping the back of her head and tugging her toward him.

She shivered, but didn't resist. His gaze focused on her moist lips, parting with anticipation as he leaned closer. With his mouth lingering a hair's breadth above hers, he murmured, "Make no mistake, we are defi-nitely seeing each other, Kylie."

He wanted to hear her admit it. Wanted her to meet him halfway, confirming that he wasn't the only one who burned with unfulfilled need.

It seemed like time froze, suspended indefinitely.

"Yes," she whispered, finally closing the gap between them and pressing her mouth against his.

Her tentative caress was like a match being tossed into a pool of gasoline.

He slanted his mouth on hers, deepening the kiss even as he pulled her closer. They were sitting on the edge of the sofa, half facing each other, but it wasn't close enough for him.

Go slow, go slow, he warned himself. But his body wasn't listening to his brain. The exotic taste of her was like a narcotic—the more he had, the more he wanted. She returned his kiss with fervor, her fingers tightly gripping his cotton shirt. His body was on fire and he longed to tear away the barrier of their clothes so he could explore every curve, every valley unen-cumbered.

When she pressed against him, his groin tightened pain-fully. Still drowning in her kiss, he smoothed his hand over her plush breast, feeling her taut, distended nipple through the soft cashmere of her purple sweater dress.

She murmured a soft, sexy sound that he wanted to believe was encouragement. But just to be certain he lifted his head and gazed down at her parted lips and flushed face.

"If we don't slow down, this won't end anytime

soon," he said. "I want you, Kylie. But I didn't bring you here for this."

Her mouth curved into a sexy smile as one eyebrow lifted. "Oh, no? You could have fooled me."

Damn. He swallowed hard, wishing for eloquence. "What I'm trying to say is that I want you, but if you're not ready to take this to the next step I'll understand." He thought it was very noble of him to give her an easy out, when every instinct in his body clamored with the need to carry her into his bedroom before she could think clearly and possibly change her mind.

He didn't want to stop.

But he didn't want to risk rushing her, or possibly hurting her even more. She'd been hurt too much in the past.

"Seth." He loved the way she said his name, in that soft, sultry voice. His stomach clenched. He feared her answer. At some level he suspected he could sway her decision by kissing her again, but he waited torturously, holding his breath. She lifted her hand to his cheek, her skin cool against his fevered skin. "I'm glad you brought me here. Because I want you, too."

Relief was dizzying. She wanted him. He had to force himself to go slow, to stand and draw her gently to her feet. He took her hand, kissed it slowly as he led her down the hall to his room.

Incredibly, she didn't hesitate when they approached his large bed. He wished he had words to tell her how special she was, how different this felt from anything he'd experienced before. She bent to reach for the hem of her sweater dress, intent on pulling it off, and he gently took the fabric from her fingers so he could do the honors. Beneath the dress she wore a matching purple lace bra and panties.

"You're so beautiful," he told her. He quickly yanked off his shirt, but when she stepped forward, reaching for his belt buckle, he froze again.

"It's—uh—been a long time for me," she confessed. He sucked in a harsh breath as the backs of her fingers brushed against the skin of his lower abdomen as the buckle slid free. She opened his fly and then pushed the pants out of her way, sliding her hands up and over his bare chest. "I might be rusty," she said, in a self-depre-cating tone.

"Never. You can't possibly know how much I want you." He cupped her face between his hands and low-ered his head to gently kiss her, trying to reassure her when words failed him.

She pressed her scantily clad body against him, her arms winding around his waist. Her skin was impossibly soft, and he nearly lost control right then and there when her hands slid beneath the waistband of his boxers, palming the curve of his derriere.

He was aching for her, his erection begging for release. He lifted her up and took the few steps to place her on the bed. Breaking off from the kiss long enough to unclasp her bra and skim her panties off, he barely had time to appreciate how beautiful her breasts were, the taut nipples begging for his mouth, when her fingers fumbled with the waistband of his boxers.

Shucking them off in a hurry, he had just enough sanity left to grab a condom from his pants pocket.

Praying she wouldn't be angry at how he'd carried them hopefully all night, he nearly swallowed his tongue when she took the packet and sheathed him herself.

He followed her down onto the bed, covering her body with his. He wanted to touch her, to kiss her everywhere, but she was urging him on, saying his name between breathy kisses. He suckled her breast, testing the softness between her thighs, finding her cleft slick and moist with desire. When she opened her legs and lifted her hips he couldn't hold off any longer.

She cried his name when he plunged deep. For a heart-wrenching moment he buried his face against her breasts, struggling to breathe. Being with Kylie like this was so perfect, and the myriad of sensations was overwhelming. He didn't want this to end too soon.

But then she slid her hands down over his back, igniting small fires everywhere she touched. He pulled back and thrust again, finding a rhythm as old as time, and both of their bodies were completely in sync as they savored the experience, seeking pleasure.

And when their release finally came, Seth realized it wasn't just their bodies that were in sync, but their hearts and souls as well.

He was falling in love with her.

CHAPTER TWELVE

KYLIE tried to ease out from beneath Seth's heavy arm draped across her waist, but he lifted his head, awakened by her movement.

"I have to go," she said regretfully. "I promised Elise I'd be home between midnight and twelve-thirty. I'm already late."

He levered upright, rubbing a hand over his chest. "I'll take you home."

"Thanks." Feeling extremely shy, which was crazy after the intimacy they'd shared, she found her discarded clothes and clutched the sweater dress in front of her, easing toward the bathroom. "I'll be ready in a few minutes."

She sensed his gaze on her as she disappeared into the adjoining bathroom, closing the door behind her. Sinking down onto the commode, she took a few minutes to pull herself together.

Seth's lovemaking had shattered her. Irrevocably changed her. She didn't know what to do or how to act. She'd morphed from a woman avoiding the complications of a man to someone who wanted more.

Everything. A future. A family.

The type of security a man like Seth wouldn't likely give her. Or any woman for that matter. No matter how much he seemed to care about her and Ben, she couldn't delude herself into thinking he was the type to settle down with a family, a minivan and two-point-five children.

Taking several deep breaths, she calmed her racing heart, and then hastily washed up before pulling her clothes back on. Finger-combing her hair as best she could, she chastised herself in the mirror.

"What? Did you really think you could casually sleep with a man without falling in love with him?" she asked her reflection.

She closed her eyes and turned away. Fool. That was exactly what she'd thought.

"Kylie?" Seth called her name, rapping on the door. "Are you all right in there?"

Drawing one last deep breath, she pasted a smile on her face before opening the door. "Of course."

He'd already dressed, and for a moment she mourned the necessity of covering up his spectacular bare chest. Instead of pulling on his discarded shirt and pants, he'd chosen soft, worn blue jeans and a sweater. He looked great, no matter what he wore.

"I wish you could stay," he murmured, drawing her close for another kiss. Her knees went weak as desire flickered to life at his touch. How did he *do* that?

She forced herself to break off the kiss, no matter how much she would have liked to start all over again. "Me, too. But, Seth, I really do need to go home."

"I know." He brushed a featherlight kiss on her

forehead and stepped back, allowing her just enough room to slip past.

He grabbed his car keys and they walked outside, back down to the parking garage. The night air was cool, and Seth cranked up the heat in Charlene when Kylie shivered, rubbing her hands over her arms.

"I have to work this weekend, Kylie," Seth told her as he drove out onto the street. "Night shift, too, which means I probably won't get a chance to see you."

The regret in his tone sounded sincere, although the impish devil on her shoulder was jeering. *See? Now that he's gotten what he wanted, he's lost interest.*

"That's all right." She forced a casual, lighthearted tone. "I have a training session scheduled for tomorrow anyway, and for several days during the week, too. We're holding our quarterly educational update and I'm teaching everyone how to use the new hypothermia unit."

"Excellent. I can't wait to see how this might impact our patient outcomes."

"Me, too." She twisted the strap of her purse as he drove, but luckily the ride to her house didn't take too long.

"You won't forget about our trip to Chicago next weekend, will you?" he asked, as he pulled into her driveway.

She had forgotten, and now regretted agreeing to go. She could try to get out of the commitment, but the thought of disappointing Ben was too much to bear. "Of course not."

"Good." He shifted the car into park and turned toward her. "I'm really looking forward to it."

"Me, too." She sensed he was going to kiss her again,

so she quickly unlatched her seat belt and opened the car door. "Good night, Seth. See you later." She got out of the car and closed Charlene's door before he could protest.

As she walked into her house, she smoothed a hand over her dress, thankful the cashmere blend didn't show wrinkles from the time it laid crumpled on the floor of Seth's bedroom.

She walked toward the living room, where she could hear the murmur of the television. "Elise? I'm home. How did everything go?"

"Great, Ms. Germaine." Elise flipped her cell phone shut when Kylie came into the room, but within a few seconds it buzzed in the teen's hand. She glanced at the display, then back up at Kylie. "Ben's a good kid. We made microwave popcorn and watched a movie."

Kylie nodded, having noticed the empty popcorn bowl sitting on the living room coffee table. She fished some money out of her purse, giving the teenager the going rate—not a bad way to earn money, an evening of talking on a cell phone and eating popcorn. "Thanks again, Elise. You can go home now."

Elise gave a distracted nod, opened her cell phone and said, "I'll call you back, Tim," before closing it again.

Kylie had to grin. "Is Tim your boyfriend?" she asked.

"Yeah." Elise glanced at Kylie, and then gestured outside the front door. "Hey, it looks like *your* boyfriend is still out there."

What? "He's not my boyfriend," she protested automatically, realizing that Elise was right. Seth hadn't driven off after she'd climbed out of his car.

A flash of panic gripped her by the throat. Why was Seth still out there? Did he think she'd let him in so they could go for another round of fabulous sex?

Would that be so bad? Yes, it would. Because she already cared about him. Too much.

Before she could change her mind, she headed out the door, pretending it was normal to see Seth, leaning back against his car. "Would you do me a favor and drive Elise home?"

His gaze bored into hers for a long moment, but then his dark gaze slid to where Elise was standing, waiting, and he nodded, as she'd hoped he would. "Sure."

"What a cool car!" Elise exclaimed as Seth opened the passenger door for her.

"Thanks, Seth." Kylie didn't stick around, but hurried back inside. Elise only lived a way up the street, and she suspected Seth might try to come straight back. She intended to be in bed, with the house dark and quiet, before that happened.

For several tense minutes she lay in her bed, waiting for Seth to knock at the front door. After a good twenty minutes of lying stiff as a board, she slowly relaxed.

Seth must have gotten her silent message, because he didn't return.

Seth didn't understand what had happened, but clearly Kylie was avoiding him.

She'd claimed she would be busy teaching classes,

but no matter what time of the day he called—morning, noon or night—she didn't pick up. He'd already left three messages without any response.

What had happened? Their evening out had been great, and the food good. The stolen hours at his condo afterward had been even better. He hadn't rushed her, had given her plenty of time to say no.

She'd come right out and admitted she wanted him, too.

So why the brush-off?

His frustration translated into a foul mood—one he tried to hide without much success. Once again, he wasn't used to this sort of reaction from a woman after a date. Especially after making love. Usually they were all over him—clingy to the point of making him claustrophobic.

At the very least they returned his freaking phone calls!

As the week wore on he became more and more short-tempered. On Thursday evening—almost a whole week since their night together—she finally returned his call.

"Hi, Seth."

"Kylie." Now that he had her on the phone he struggled with what to say. Should he demand an explanation as to why she was avoiding him? Or play it cool? This gnawing uncertainty as to how to approach a woman was new to him.

And he didn't like it.

"I'm glad you called," he said at last. "I wanted to finalize our plans for the weekend."

"Sure. What time would you like us to be ready?"

When she didn't immediately tell him she'd changed

her mind about going, as he'd feared, he breathed a little easier. So far, so good. He cleared his throat. "I thought we'd meet at three-thirty and drive into Milwaukee to get something to eat before taking the six-thirty train down to Chicago."

"Sounds like a plan. Ben is totally excited about this trip."

Just Ben? Was that why she hadn't called off their plans? Because she didn't want to disappoint her son? If he knew one thing about Kylie, it was that she'd always put her son's needs before her own.

Always.

"How has your week been?" he asked, trying not to assume the worst because he hadn't heard from her in so long.

"Busy. I finished all the training sessions this week," she admitted. "You'll be glad to know our hypothermia protocol is officially in use."

"That's good news." Seth couldn't help thinking about how far his relationship with Kylie had come since that first day they'd met just a few weeks ago. She'd been so adamant about not sharing a meal with him, and now they'd progressed to making love.

But relationships were new territory for him. He didn't understand why things weren't going as well as they should. He felt as if Kylie were slipping away.

He didn't want to lose her.

His fingers tightened on the phone, and he wished he could see the expression on her face, gauge the unspoken emotion in her pretty green eyes. "Kylie, I've missed you this past week. Very much."

There was a brief pause. "I missed you, too," she finally admitted in a soft voice. "But honestly, I really have been busy, Seth. Ben needed all sorts of new clothes for school, not to mention a boatload of school supplies. Between Ben and the quarterly training sessions I didn't have a single minute to spare."

"I understand." He relaxed a bit, realizing maybe her lack of response had been justified. She was a single mother. Between working and having sole responsibility for Ben he understood she didn't have a lot of extra time on her hands.

Had his father felt this same frustration upon meeting his mother, whose time had been taken up by not just one but three kids?

"I promise you'll have a relaxing weekend," he assured her. "I'll see you Saturday at three-thirty, okay?"

"Right. Saturday at three-thirty. We'll both be ready."

Seth hung up the phone, barely glancing at his pager vibrating madly on his waist.

He'd see Kylie on Saturday.

But they wouldn't be alone. Ben would be with them.

Thinking about how much Ben would love attending the game made him grin, yet at the same time he couldn't help wishing for more time to be alone with Kylie.

Because somehow he didn't think stealing a few hours together at night in his hotel room while Ben was sleeping in her room was going to be an option.

Seth saw Kylie sooner than he'd anticipated—when she brought in a patient the following morning.

"Sixty-two-year-old man found by a neighbor after

he fell off his ladder while trying to clean the leaves out of his gutters." Kylie's expression was tense, serious. "The patient is Chuck Rigby, and he has a significant history of poorly controlled adult onset diabetes."

Chuck? He knew Chuck Rigby and so did Kylie. She'd told him Chuck had run into problems in the past when he hadn't taken his insulin. "How are his vital signs?"

"Not good. His blood pressure is low, less than ninety systolic, and his heart rate is high. I've been afraid to give too much fluid, though, because he's not responding and his pupils are unequal. The right is larger than the left."

"Let's run a full set of labs and get a large bore catheter in place so we can monitor him more closely. Kylie, do you think it's possible he forgot to take his insulin again?" Falling off the ladder would be the case of the head injury, but he couldn't discount the possibility of hyperglycemia, either.

"I did a fingerstick glucose on the way over. His serum glucose was extremely high at 853."

"Do we have any idea what his current daily dose of insulin is?" he asked.

Kylie nodded. "I remember from last time. He usually takes thirty units of NovoLog insulin each morning."

"Give him the same dose now," Seth instructed, glad that Kylie had such a good memory. It saved him from digging through Chuck's medical records. "We're also going to need a CT scan of his head, not to mention X-rays to rule out other fractures."

"Someone needs to get in touch with his wife, Estelle," Kylie said. "She must have already left for work by the time he fell."

"I'll have the social worker place the call."

Kylie put a hand on his arm. "I'd rather do it."

He hesitated, and then nodded. "Don't say too much. The last thing she needs is to get hurt rushing over here."

"I know."

While Kylie was on the phone, Alyssa called him over. "Seth? I think Chuck is waking up."

With relief he saw that Chuck was indeed starting to wake up. They'd still need that CT of his head, but at least now he knew that a portion of his lethargy was related to the out-of-control diabetes.

When Chuck's wife Estelle showed up, about ten minutes later, he was grateful he'd be able to give her cautiously optimistic news. But he stressed how it was possible the fall was related to his poorly controlled diabetes, and that it was important for Chuck to get his diabetes under control or next time he might not be so lucky.

Kylie echoed his sentiments, before packing up her stretcher to take it back out to the paramedic rig. He followed her outside for a moment.

"Nice work on remembering the insulin dose," he said.

"Thanks." She blushed, and he liked the way she took the smallest compliment to heart. "We have to run, but I'll see you tomorrow."

"Tomorrow," he echoed, stepping back, knowing he was needed inside. "Bye, Kylie."

Even if he wouldn't be able to share a hotel room with her, he was still looking forward to their weekend together.

A little too much for his peace of mind.

* * *

Kylie wanted to scream when Ben asked for the fif-teenth time when Dr. Seth would arrive.

"Ben, constantly asking me when he's coming isn't going to make him show up any sooner." She tried to soften her words with a smile. "Why don't you go outside and play with Joey for a while? You'll see Dr. Seth drive up in his car, I'm sure."

"Okay." Ben ran out of the house, letting the door slam behind him.

She rubbed her temples, wondering if Ben was more excited about the football game or seeing Seth again. For herself, she didn't know what she wanted. She looked forward to seeing Seth, but at the same time she knew the situation between them was impossible.

She'd used being busy as an excuse to avoid him all this week. The reality of running around doing all the mundane chores of parenthood made her realize Seth didn't really have a clue what her life was like. If Tristan hadn't stayed to help raise his own son, why would Seth take on that responsibility?

She simply couldn't imagine it. Especially when Seth had been so upset by finding out his dad wasn't his bio-logical father. So they'd remain friends. No matter how much she longed for more.

Glancing inside the duffel bag one more time, to make sure she had everything they were going to need, she zipped it closed and took it outside to her trunk. They'd have to take her car, since Charlene didn't have a back-seat.

Inside the house, she found herself pacing, waiting almost as impatiently as Ben for Seth to arrive. At five minutes to four she heard a car drive up the driveway. She took a moment to double-check her reflection in the mirror over the bathroom sink before going out to meet him.

On the porch, she stopped when she noticed a navy blue four-door sensible sedan parked in her driveway. She frowned. Had someone else stopped by?

"Hi, Kylie." Seth was standing beside Ben.

"Seth, where's Charlene?"

"I sold her to a friend of mine."

She stared. Had she heard right? "You *sold* her? Why?"

He lifted a negligent shoulder, flashing a lopsided grin. "Simon coveted Charlene from the moment I bought her. He offered a fair price and I took it. It's better to have something a little more practical anyway."

Practical? Since when did Seth care about practical?

"I—uh—already put our stuff in my trunk," she said, trying to gather her scattered thoughts.

"I'll take care of it." He chatted with Ben as he moved their overnight cases from her old, dependable car to the trunk of his new one.

Her heart fluttered painfully.

He'd sold his racy sports car. Was this a sign that Seth was ready for a more serious relationship after all?

CHAPTER THIRTEEN

"I BOUGHT something for you."

Kylie stared in surprise at the bag Seth dropped in her lap. He started the car and then glanced at her expectantly.

"For me?" Since the name on the bag advertised the name of a local retail store, she knew what she'd find inside. She smiled as she pulled out the shirt. "A Green Bay Packers jersey?"

"And a Bears jersey, too," Seth quickly interjected, when Ben protested loudly from his perch in the backseat. "This way you can root for either team, depending on who happens to be winning."

She laughed, already feeling torn between Seth's Packers and Ben's Bears. "Maybe I should cheer for a different team altogether?"

"Not the Vikings, Mom. They stink."

She shot a warning look over her shoulder at Ben. "Watch your language," she chided, before turning back around to the front. The interior of Seth's car smelled brand-new, as if he'd just driven it off the lot. She still couldn't believe he'd bought a new car.

And not just any new car.

A family car. A four-door sedan.

"So, are you going to name this one, too?" she asked, smoothing her hand over the plush fabric of the seat cushion. The car might not be sporty, but it certainly didn't lack any luxury.

"Yeah, I already have." Seth shot her a cheeky grin. "Suzanne."

"Suzanne?" She raked the interior with a skeptical glance. The car didn't scream Suzanne to her.

But then she wasn't a guy.

"Why not?" Seth asked, heading for the interstate highway. "She's sleek, classy. As soon as I saw her I knew she was a Suzanne."

"Did your father name his cars, too?" she asked, trying to understand this weird tendency to humanize his possessions.

"Nah. That was something Caleb and I started, after reading Stephen King's classic, *Christine*."

Good grief—he'd named his car after reading a horror novel? "That's sick."

He gave a negligent shrug. "Caleb and I wanted to see if our cars would come to life, like Christine, but they didn't."

"And a good thing, since the Christine in Stephen King's novel tried to kill its owner," she said in an exasperated tone. She would like to meet Seth's brother. And his sister, Tess. But clearly, Seth didn't think their relationship was at the point where he'd consider introducing her to his family.

Would he ever take that step? A more drastic move than simply buying a new car? She wasn't sure.

When they reached Milwaukee, Seth pulled into a family-style restaurant—one that was completely opposite from the place they'd eaten dinner at last weekend. She sent him an appreciative glance, knowing there would be a decent children's menu for Ben to choose from.

She decided to try the grilled salmon, while Seth settled on a large burger.

"Gee, have a little chicken with your ketchup," Seth teased as Ben drowned his chicken strips in the red sauce until he could barely see them. "Why did you get chicken strips if you don't like how they taste?"

"I like how they taste with ketchup," Ben said, jamming one in his mouth, smearing a red streak across his cheek.

"Help! Help! He's not breathing!"

Huh? Kylie exchanged a look with Seth and they both jumped to their feet, glancing over to where a man was slumped over on the table.

They rushed over. "Call 911," Kylie told the hovering waitress, who was staring at the man helplessly.

Seth eased the man onto the floor, stretching him out so they could work. Kylie knelt on the opposite side of the unconscious man. "Heart attack?"

"That would be my guess." Seth opened the man's airway, bending his head to listen and feel for breathing. Kylie took a few minutes to rush back over to her purse for the face shield resuscitation mask she carried with her at all times.

She'd never had to use it until now.

"Here." She spread it out over the man's mouth to protect Seth.

"No spontaneous breathing and no pulse," he confirmed. "We'll need to start CPR."

Kylie found her landmarks on the man's chest, and then began giving chest compressions, even as she glanced over to keep track of Ben. He'd followed them, and stood near the table, watching them work on the patient with wide eyes. She counted out loud for Seth's sake, hoping the resuscitation wasn't too traumatic for her six-year-old to handle.

"Are you getting tired?" Seth asked, after they'd completed several minutes of CPR.

She nodded, indicating it was time to switch. When chest compressions were done correctly, with the proper depth and pressure, they were physically taxing. She'd learned the hard way in the field that staying with chest compressions too long had the potential to harm the patient.

Seth was going strong at chest compressions when the paramedic crew showed up. She was pleased to see that they carried the same hypothermia unit she'd just trained her team on.

She slid out of the way so the paramedic could place an Ambu bag connected to an oxygen tank over the man's mouth, to provide him with more effective breathing. Falling into the rhythm of her job, she helped place ECG electrodes on the man's chest.

"Seth is an ED physician," Kylie explained to the paramedics as they turned on the defibrillator. "So go ahead and use the manual mode."

The paramedic nodded. Seth stopped compressions and they all stared at the monitor.

"V-fib. Let's get ready to shock at one hundred joules," Seth ordered. The paramedic pushed the button, and when that shock wasn't enough to help change the underlying rhythm Seth ordered a second shock. This time the treatment worked, converting their patient into a normal sinus rhythm.

"Nice job," Seth said. "I think you'd better get him ready for transport."

Kylie helped connect the hypothermia machine as the paramedic spread the cooling blanket over the patient. After all the excitement, watching them wheel the patient away was rather anticlimactic.

"My first time using the hypothermia unit and I'm not even at work so I can follow the patient's progress," Kylie said in a dejected tone. She hoped their quick response, along with the new hypothermia protocol, would help increase the guy's chances of survival.

"Is that man going to die?" Ben asked.

Oh, dear. She'd almost forgotten about her son. She bent over to give Ben a reassuring hug. "No, Ben, he's not going to die. In fact, thanks to our quick work, he should do pretty well."

"Really?" Ben didn't look convinced. She glanced helplessly at Seth, seeking advice. Had this been too traumatic for him?

"Your mom is telling the truth, Ben." Seth took Ben's hand and led him back to their table. "We were able to save that man's life because we offered help right away. This is what doctors like me and paramedics like your mom do all day. We help people get better when they're sick."

"Like when I was hurt?" Ben asked.

"Exactly."

Kylie's heart did a funny little flip when Seth smiled at Ben. She reminded herself not to read too much into Seth's actions. He was nice to everyone. "Don't be upset about what happened. Let's just finish our dinner."

The restaurant manager came over and offered to bring them fresh meals, since their food had grown cold. He also thanked them profusely for their help. Embarrassed, Seth brushed off the gratitude, but he did take the offer of fresh dinners.

The extra wait, though, meant they had to rush to the train station.

In Chicago they took a taxi cab, thrilling Ben with a novel experience, and they arrived at their hotel much later than they'd planned. Ben was yawning from all the excitement, keeping his eyes open with an effort.

Kylie opened the door to her room, glancing over at Seth, who occupied the room right next door. "Good night, Seth."

"Good night, Kylie, Ben." He stood in the hallway, watching as they entered the room. "Just knock if you need anything," he added in a low tone.

Kylie suspected Seth was subtly suggesting she could sneak out and come over to his room once Ben was asleep. And she had to admit the idea was tempting—at least on a personal level.

If she were honest, she'd admit she'd used needing to get ready for Ben's first week of school and all the errands she'd needed to do as an excuse to avoid facing him. Not just because it had been proof he didn't fit into her life, but because she cared about Seth too much. She couldn't have an intimate relationship with a guy like Seth when it wasn't just her heart but her son's that she needed to consider.

But then Seth had showed up in a new car. Was she overdramatizing his motives? Maybe Seth had simply grown tired of Charlene? Choosing a sensible sedan might not mean much.

It wasn't as if he'd declared undying love for her.

And that was the problem, she realized. She'd made love with Seth and she didn't even know how he really felt about her. Sure, he cared. But what did that mean? Did he think they'd just keep seeing each other when they had time, sharing spectacular sex without any plans for the future?

Maybe. Since Seth had told her from the beginning he avoided planning for the future.

She let out a heavy sigh. Going to Seth's room right now wasn't a smart idea, since she suspected Seth didn't want to spend their time together discussing their relationship and where it was going. And she didn't want to argue.

She'd come on this trip because she hadn't wanted to disappoint Ben. A football game was hardly a romantic date.

Best to keep this trip light, since it was for Ben's benefit after all. Continuing a romantic intimacy when they didn't have a future wasn't something she was willing to do.

The next morning they ate Sunday brunch in the hotel restaurant, and Kylie was relieved Seth didn't seem upset about her decision to stay in her own room all night. At least he treated her no differently than before.

They walked the short distance to the stadium, along with hundreds of other football fans. Once they were seated, Kylie glanced around, awed by the intense energy level pulsing through the crowd. Music blared from loudspeakers and fans leaped to their feet, cheering madly when the players were introduced. The team played to the crowd, waving as they ran out onto the field.

Seth was right. Watching the game from the stands was totally different from seeing it on the television. The players lived for the reactions from the crowd, and the fans didn't disappoint them. The plays were a little hard to follow, but the hits the players took were loud enough to make her wince.

The Bears were winning, and she found herself rooting for them with Ben, screaming until their voices were hoarse as the Packers tied the game with only two minutes left to play.

"Hey, buddy, you might want to divorce your wife and disown your kid if they're going to root for the Bears."

She glanced at the Packers fan who'd addressed Seth, wondering if the guy wearing green and gold from head to toe might have ingested a few too many beers.

"We're not married," Kylie replied tartly.

Seth tried to play along. "I've been trying to convert them from the dark side," he joked. "But so far no luck."

"If you're not married, then run while you can," the guy advised, as the Bears took the kickoff and ran a good fifteen yards down the field.

Seth simply shook his head, his gaze locked on the field as the Bears managed to get another first down. Kylie knew the Packers fan was only kidding, but she couldn't help realizing her differences with Seth were more than just which team they chose to support. They were so different in other ways, too.

Her annoyance faded as the Bears continued to move the ball down the field. When there were only ten seconds left on the play clock, the Bears team set up for a field goal.

"They're going to choke," Seth warned Ben.

"No, they're not." Ben was practically jumping from one foot to the other with excitement. Seth lifted him up, setting his feet on the back of the seat in front of them so he could see better.

The kick was good. The crowd went wild as the Bears won the game by three points.

"Maybe you should start rooting for the Bears," Kylie told Seth as they waited for the crowd to thin before heading back over to the hotel, where they'd left their luggage.

"Never," Seth said, although his tone lacked emphasis.

They walked back to the hotel to fetch their luggage, and then took a cab back to the train station. Once they arrived in Milwaukee, they picked up some fast food to eat on the ride home to Cedar Bluff.

Ben was half asleep in the backseat, dozing off, and then blinking to wake up. Kylie knew the excitement of the game had worn him out.

"Thanks for taking us to the game," she said quietly. "I know Ben will remember this day for a long time."

Seth grinned. "Yeah, especially since his team won."

The day *had* been special, but not because Ben's team had won. There was a part of her that had liked them being together, as if they were a family. Ben had reveled in Seth's attention, and she knew her son secretly longed for a father.

If things didn't work out with Seth, Ben would be hurt. Badly.

Seth had never once mentioned raising Ben as his own son, the same way Gregory Taylor had raised him. That was a lot to ask of any man.

"Kylie?" Seth reached over to take her hand, and kept his voice low so as not to wake Ben. "Do you think you could find a babysitter for some night this week?"

Her heart betrayed her by racing erratically in her chest. "I don't know, but I can try."

"I'm working days all week," Seth said. "So any night is open."

"Sure." She glanced over her shoulder at Ben, making sure he was still sleeping. "We should probably talk."

"Talking is fine." He gently squeezed her hand. "But I was thinking about doing more than just talking."

She bit her lip and tried to smile as he pulled into the driveway. Somehow she wasn't sure there would be any more togetherness once they talked.

Because once Seth realized she was looking for something permanent, like a future, she suspected he might choose to walk away.

Seth mulled over his weekend with Kylie and Ben as he worked on Monday. All in all, despite the fact that Kylie hadn't come knocking on his door like he'd hoped, he thought the outing had been a huge success.

Kylie had seemed a little distant, but he thought

maybe the reason was because she hadn't wanted to be overly affectionate in front of her son. He wasn't a parent, but he could somewhat understand. Hugging and kissing a guy would be difficult for her to explain to a six-year-old.

His gut had tightened, though, when she'd told him she wanted to talk. He generally avoided women who wanted to talk. Women usually only wanted to talk when things weren't going well.

He turned his attention to the job at hand, which consisted of a young soccer player who'd been brought in with a twisted ankle. "Doug, you'll need to stay off your ankle for at least a week," he instructed. "The nurse is going to fit you with a pair of crutches to use."

"Crutches? For a whole week?" Doug's horrified expression indicated he thought this was a fate worse than death. "But that means I'll miss the next game!"

He understood. The Cedar Bluff High School soccer team was headed for the championship. They'd won it last year. "I'm sorry, but you'll only hurt yourself worse if you don't do as I say. Don't risk your entire future for one game," he advised, before leaving the room to find a nurse.

Alyssa usually worked in the trauma room, but today she'd been assigned to the ED area. But where was she now? Alyssa had been quieter than usual lately, and, while they were close, Alyssa was one of the few women he hadn't dated. He thought there was definitely something bothering her.

He found another nurse to do Doug's patient discharge teaching, then checked on the progress of an elderly patient who was waiting to be admitted for a severe kidney infection, satisfied to overhear the nurse was giving a report to the floor.

Fifteen minutes later, he still hadn't found Alyssa. Odd, because she was one of the best trauma nurses in the entire ED, and it wasn't like her to simply disappear, leaving her work to others. Not that they were terribly busy, but still...

He headed back toward the staff lounge. The muffled sounds of crying reached him before he saw her, curled up in the corner, her face buried against the sofa cushion.

Had someone died? He remembered all too well the feeling of overwhelming helplessness after his mother had passed away so unexpectedly. One minute she'd been healthy as could be, planning for the upcoming arrival of Caleb's new baby, and the next she was gone.

Alarmed, he crossed over to her. "Alyssa, what is it? Are you okay? What's wrong?"

She lifted her face, looking embarrassed as she swiped the tears from her cheeks. "It's nothing. I'm fine."

Yeah, and he was the King of Siam. "You're not fine. You're upset." Sobbing women made him uncomfortable, and he sensed she wanted privacy but he couldn't just leave her like this.

"Don't mind me. I'm just being stupid." She sniffled loudly and swiped her face again.

He stood, uncertainly. "Do you want to talk about it?"

"Not really." Her pathetic attempt to smile tugged at his heart. "I—uh—don't suppose you know where Jadon is, do you? He left town, and his cell phone is no longer in service."

Jadon? Now Alyssa's crying made sense. Jadon

Reichert had been one of his colleagues—not exactly a close friend, since Jadon had been out of town a lot, but a good doctor. Jadon had left rather unexpectedly for good two months ago, wreaking havoc on their schedule. Alyssa had been close to Jadon during the time he was here. Obviously Seth hadn't realized just how close.

"No, I'm sorry. I don't know where he went." *Damn.* Jadon must not have told Alyssa, either, the jerk. And here she was sobbing as if her heart was crushed. "What happened? Did you guys have a fight? Is that why he left?"

"No fight. Not really." She sighed again, and he was relieved to see her crying jag was over. "I really don't know why he left. But never mind. It's my problem, not yours."

Maybe, but seeing Alyssa so obviously distressed bothered him. She looked just like his mother had after his father had died—purely miserable.

He went back to work, finishing off his shift, but he couldn't ignore the sick feeling in his stomach.

Love had the power to hurt. Badly. He put a hand to the center of his chest, rubbing the imaginary ache building there. Was he crazy to think about a future with Kylie? To think about being a surrogate father to Ben? What if something happened to either of them? How would he survive?

His mother had tried to hide the extent of her deep sorrow after his father's death, but he'd always known it was there. The light had vanished from her eyes, and though she'd never said anything about it he'd known she was lonely. And then, after she was gone, he'd discovered she'd lost not just one man in her life but two.

Twice married and twice widowed.

Was the risk of falling in love with someone worth the eventual pain of losing them? Suddenly he wasn't so sure he wanted to find out.

The best thing might be to break things off with Kylie—before it was too late.

CHAPTER FOURTEEN

SETH went home that night, intending to call Kylie, but when his cell phone rang the moment he walked in the door he realized she'd managed to beat him to it.

"Hi, Kylie." He greeted her cautiously.

"Hey, Seth. I arranged for a babysitter for tomorrow night, if that's still okay with you?"

The sound of her husky voice brought back memories of the heated lovemaking they'd shared. Despite the tightening of his groin, the sick feeling in his stomach intensified at the realization she might be planning an intimate evening.

After all, he'd hinted at making love again, hadn't he?

"Tomorrow night would be great." He forced the words past his tight throat. "I'm looking forward to it."

His tone must not have sounded totally convincing, since there was a brief pause before she asked, "About six?"

"Sure, I'll pick you up then." He flipped his phone shut and battled the urge to toss the stupid thing against the wall. He was angry and upset. But not with Kylie or Ben. They were the innocent victims here.

He was angry with himself, for ignoring his own rules. *This* was the reason he'd always kept his love life light and friendly. This pain. The deep, piercing agony that already tightened his chest and made his head ache.

He felt sick to his stomach.

The next day time moved at warp speed—probably because he was dreading the date he'd arranged with Kylie. The thought of sitting through a dinner at a restaurant held no appeal, and since he was running late anyway he decided to pick up some deli sandwiches to go. They could eat in Cedar Bluff Park, at the highest point overlooking Lake Michigan. That way they wouldn't need to worry about being distracted by waiters or other diners possibly overhearing their conversation.

And sitting on the bluff for sure meant no lovemaking.

As if she'd sensed his intent to keep this date casual, Kylie arrived in form-fitting blue jeans and a soft V-necked sweater in deep purple. His mouth went dry and he purposely avoided looking at the enticing hint of cleavage her sweater displayed.

"Something smells good," she commented as she slid into Suzanne's passenger seat.

"I brought deli sandwiches. Thought it would be nice to go up to the picnic spot on the bluff overlooking Lake Michigan."

"Great. I've heard the view is awesome, but I haven't been up there."

The way she avoided his gaze warned him she knew exactly what he planned to do. Overwhelming guilt gnawed on his insides, burning his stomach lining like acid.

He parked in the lot, and then reached into the backseat to grab the food before following Kylie up the path leading to the top of the bluff.

"Wow," she whispered when they crested the top of the bluff. "Impressive."

"Cedar Bluff, the town, was named after James Cedar—the guy who founded it," he informed her. "These bluffs were formed when the glacier moved through the area thousands of years ago."

She stared for a long moment at the waves rippling over the lake's surface, before turning toward him. "Seth, I'm sorry. But I can't do this. I can't see you anymore."

He was so shocked that he could only stare at her. The fact that he'd planned to break things off himself didn't matter in the least. "Why?"

"Because I need more than just having fun with you. I need it all. A husband, a true father to help raise Ben. I'm sorry, but I'm not cut out for a casual fling."

Casual fling? He let the bag of deli sandwiches drop to the sandy soil at his feet so he could grasp her arms. "Kylie, how could you think I feel *casual* toward you? For God's sake, woman, I love you."

Her glorious green eyes widened at his declaration, and suddenly he understood she was running away from him the same way he'd intended to run from her. From the threat of their love.

A spark of anger burned. Running away? Well, hell. He wasn't a coward and neither was she. Love hurt when the person you loved was gone. So what? Did that mean if Kylie walked away right now he'd hurt any less?

No. And really love didn't have to hurt. Love could be full of life and laughter, too. His parents had been happy during the time they were together. He knew his mother hadn't regretted a moment of her marriage to his father. Probably hadn't regretted either marriage.

"Seth, don't." She tried to tug out of his grip. "I have to think about Ben."

"Ben? Is that really why you're running away?" He seriously doubted it. "Kylie, I had an awesome father, who raised me as his own. He was incredibly patient as he taught me how to play football. I asked him how he knew so much about sports, and do you know what he said?" She shook her head. "He said, 'When I first met your mother I didn't know anything about sports, but I knew I had to learn quick since I had two active sons to keep busy.'"

"Your father sounds like a wonderful man."

"He was. And I think I can learn to be a good father, too. I realize now that my father was brave enough to learn how to be a father to us kids. I'm more than willing to do the same thing. To learn how to be a husband to you and a father to Ben."

"And what if you decide a few years down the road that you don't want to be a husband anymore?" Kylie pulled her hands from his and half turned away, raking a hand through her hair, straightening the strands that had been tousled from the breeze. "Seth, parenthood isn't all fun—especially once the novelty wears off. I know you're going to eventually decide to move on to someone else."

He couldn't believe what he was hearing. Kylie didn't believe him. Didn't trust him. Didn't trust in his love for her.

And other than shouting it out over the lake, so the whole world could hear him, he didn't know how to convince her.

Kylie stood at the edge of the bluff, gazing at the deep blue water and wishing she knew what to do.

Seth claimed he loved her. He claimed he wanted to be a husband and a father. And she didn't doubt that he sincerely meant it. But there was far more to having a family than buying a new car.

He had no clue what he was in for. Had no inkling of what it was like to be up all night with a sick baby, or a toddler with the flu. When Ben had gotten hit by the car, her entire life had teetered on the edge until she'd discovered he was all right.

"So that's it, then?" Seth's tone was bitter. "You're going to refuse to trust me? You're just going to walk away?"

She licked her dry lips, feeling sick. "This isn't about trust. It's about knowing what's best." He didn't understand that her life was mundane, boring. The risk was too great to make a mistake. She wouldn't be the only one to suffer if things went wrong.

Ben would suffer, too.

He let out a harsh sound. "This is about trust. You could choose to believe me, to take a chance on us. On love."

Tears welled in her eyes, but she still shook her head.

Seth's mouth tightened. "You know what's really

funny? I actually brought you here to break off our relationship because I loved you too much. I was too afraid of how hurt I'd be if I ever lost you. The way my mother lost not just one husband but two."

Confused, she stared at him, trying to understand his rather warped logic.

"And yet the irony of the situation is that you're walking away from me because you don't love me enough." His hurt expression sliced deep.

That wasn't true. She *did* love him. Too much.

So why couldn't she trust that he actually loved her in return?

She took a deep breath and let it out slowly, trying to combat a sudden dizziness. "I think I need to sit down."

Instantly his face registered concern. "Are you okay? Maybe we should have eaten first. You look pale. Come on, sit down on this bench."

With his hand under her elbow, she crossed over to the park bench where they'd planned to eat their dinner. Except she wasn't the least bit hungry.

"Do you need something? I think there are some soft drinks in this bag." He reached for the deli dinner that they'd ignored and pulled a can of lemonade out of the sack. "Here, try this."

His kind consideration after the bitter argument they'd just had hit her hard.

Dear God. What if Seth was telling the truth? What if he really did love her?

She took a hasty gulp of the lemonade, coughing a bit to clear her throat. "Seth? I need you to answer one question."

His gaze was wary, but he nodded. "All right."

"I need to know why. *Why* do you love me?" She was ashamed to admit that maybe it was her own lack of self-confidence that made it difficult to believe. "You could have any woman at Cedar Bluff Hospital—heck, any woman in the entire town—but you think you love me."

"Ah. I think I understand. You're afraid I'm going to be like Ben's father—leaving you when you and Ben needed him the most. Is that it?"

She lifted her shoulder helplessly. "Maybe. I don't know. I guess I just don't understand why you love me. I'm nothing special."

Seth frowned and shook his head. "That's where you're wrong, Kylie. You're very special. But I think the biggest part of the reason I love you is that you don't have a clue how beautiful, smart, hard-working, dedicated and unselfish you really are."

"Seth, stop exaggerating. I'm serious."

"So am I." He let out an exasperated sigh. "Kylie, you're asking me to put my feelings into words and I'm trying. But it's not easy." He sat next to her and took her hand in his. "When I first met you I was attracted to your physical beauty, which is spectacular, but even then I was equally attracted to the person you were on the inside. Not only were you smart enough to pick up on Marilyn's heart attack diagnosis, but you were also brave enough to stand your ground with a senior para-medic who clearly doubted you. The more I got to know you, the more there was to admire. You always insisted on putting your son first. You resisted any interference in the life you'd planned out for you and your son, which drove me crazy as much as I respected it. Yet you quickly learned to care about the people in this town, including Chuck and Estelle—who are doing fine, by the way, now that they're taking diabetes education classes."

She shifted uncomfortably on the bench. "But, Seth, anyone would do those things."

"No, they wouldn't," he corrected her softly. "And even if they did, no one else does them like you. But do you want to know the real reason I fell in love with you?"

She nodded.

"Because you remind me of my mother." He must have noticed the horrified expression in her eyes, because he quickly interjected, "Not physically, Kylie, for heaven's sake. Emotionally. Your love for Ben, your willingness to try new things, like a football game in a crowded stadium, your love of life. Your respect for others." His smile was crooked. "Kylie, I can't think of any other woman I'd want to be the mother of my children. There isn't anyone else I want standing by my side through the good times and especially through the difficult times. I love you. I need you. I don't know what else I can say to convince you."

She gently placed her finger over his mouth. "You don't have to say any more. I believe you, Seth, because I love you, too. And I'm not sure I could explain why half as eloquently as you just did."

"Thank God," he murmured, pulling her close into his arms. The gesture was somewhat awkward as they were seated side by side on the bench. He tugged her around until she was in his lap, her feet dangling off the end of the park bench.

She leaned forward and kissed him, needing—no,

craving this physical connection. Secure in the strength of his arms, with his mouth slanted over hers, making her dizzy with desire, she wondered how she could have ever doubted him.

He loved her. Almost as much as she loved him.

It was a long time before Seth reluctantly lifted his head. "Kylie, this bench isn't going to work for what I'd like to do with you."

She laughed, disentangling herself from his embrace, shivering a bit as the wind kicked up, significantly dropping the temperature. She tried to keep her teeth from chattering. "Well, I don't think Suzanne's backseat is going to be much better."

He lifted a brow and leered. "Wanna bet?"

The mischievous glint in his eye reminded her of the first day they'd met, when he'd made it clear he wanted her.

"Come on." He grabbed her hand, and took another moment to snag the bag of food off the soft ground before dragging her toward the car.

Giggling, she crowded into the backseat with him, barely able to close the door against the buffeting wind. "See?" She shoved her tangled hair away from her face with a grimace. "I told you. We hardly have room to sit back here, much less do anything else."

"Kylie, what happened to your spirit of adventure?" Seth chided softly.

He angled back so he was leaning against the door, and pulled her up so she was lying on top of him. She could feel his blunt arousal through the multiple layers of their clothes.

He kissed her again, slower, deeper, until her resistance melted away, transitioning into urgent need. There wasn't nearly enough room—their elbows were bumping against the door and their knees hitting the back of the seat cushion—but suddenly she didn't care. She wanted Seth—right here, right now.

It wasn't until much later, when they'd finally straightened out their clothes and dug in the bag of food for something to eat, that she turned to him.

"So tell me the truth. Is sex in the backseat the real reason you traded Charlene in for Suzanne?"

He grinned, that sexy, lethal grin, and shook his head, leaning over to give her a hard kiss. "No. I traded Charlene in for Suzanne because somewhere deep down I knew I wanted a family with you. Sex in the backseat just happens to be an added side benefit—like having malted milk powder sprinkled on a hot fudge sundae."

She'd never tried a sundae with malted milk powder sprinkled on top. "Except once we're married we won't have to squeeze back here like this," she pointed out.

"I didn't ask you to marry me yet."

She froze, a horrible icy fear creeping over her. *What?* How could she have possibly misunderstood?

"Kylie, I think I need to talk to Ben first—to make sure he's all right with me marrying you." Seth glanced at her, his gaze completely serious. "Don't you think?"

"Yes." She managed to find her voice. "I think that asking Ben first would be perfect."

"Well, then, hurry up and eat so we can get back before his bedtime."

She laughed, and took another bite of her cold roast

beef sandwich. There was absolutely no question in her mind as to how Ben would respond to Seth's question.

She was the luckiest woman in the world to have not one but two wonderful men in her life.

Seth sat across from Ben at Kylie's kitchen table, feeling unaccountably nervous. What in the world had he been thinking? How could he possibly have left the fate of his future in a six-year-old's hands?

Kylie's reassuring smile helped a little.

He cleared his throat. "Ben, what would you think if I asked your mom to marry me?"

Ben eyed him suspiciously over the rim of his glass of milk. "Why do you want to marry her?"

"Because I love her. And I love you. If I marry your mom the three of us can be a family."

"So you'd live here with us forever?" The excited glint in Ben's eyes made the tension ease out of his shoulders.

"Yes. I'd be your dad and live with you forever."

"Cool. I've always wanted a dad."

Seth glanced at Kylie, who blinked away tears, then back at Ben. His own voice was husky with emotion. "Good, because I always wanted a little boy like you, too."

There was a long pause as Seth realized this was it. This was his new family. And he wasn't afraid. In fact, he felt pretty darn good.

He planned on making Gregory Taylor proud of him.

"Well," Kylie said brightly, "I guess that's settled, then. Ben, finish your milk and then go brush your teeth."

"Aw, can't I stay up a little later? Please?" Ben pleaded, looking straight at Seth.

Oh, boy. He was in trouble. The kid was already trying to get his way by playing the old parent against the new parent.

"Listen to your mother," he told Ben, as he stood and crossed over to Kylie. He drew her up and put his arm around her, adding, "And when I'm your dad, you'd better listen to me, too."

"All right." Ben sighed and walked toward the doorway.

Seth was glad Ben had listened—at least this time—although he was sure there'd be other challenges down the road. He pulled Kylie close, covering her mouth in a soft kiss.

"Hey, no kissing!" Ben called over his shoulder, his expression mirroring his disgust.

Seth raised his head and grinned. "Sorry, Ben, but there is absolutely going to be kissing. And you may as well be prepared for babies, too."

Kylie choked on a laugh, hiding her face against his neck.

"Babies?" Ben grimaced, and then let out another heavy sigh. "Okay, but I only want boy babies. A little brother to play with could be fun."

Seth shook his head, glancing down at Kylie—the woman who held his heart, life and soul in her tender yet capable hands. "Actually, I'm open to either. But I'd especially like a girl baby—just like your mom."

0709 Gen Std HB

ROMANCE

Desert Prince, Bride of Innocence	Lynne Graham
Raffaele: Taming His Tempestuous Virgin	Sandra Marton
The Italian Billionaire's Secretary Mistress	Sharon Kendrick
Bride, Bought and Paid For	Helen Bianchin
Hired for the Boss's Bedroom	Cathy Williams
The Christmas Love-Child	Jennie Lucas
Mistress to the Merciless Millionaire	Abby Green
Italian Boss, Proud Miss Prim	Susan Stephens
Proud Revenge, Passionate Wedlock	Janette Kenny
The Buenos Aires Marriage Deal	Maggie Cox
Betrothed: To the People's Prince	Marion Lennox
The Bridesmaid's Baby	Barbara Hannay
The Greek's Long-Lost Son	Rebecca Winters
His Housekeeper Bride	Melissa James
A Princess for Christmas	Shirley Jump
The Frenchman's Plain-Jane Project	Myrna Mackenzie
Italian Doctor, Dream Proposal	Margaret McDonagh
Marriage Reunited: Baby on the Way	Sharon Archer

HISTORICAL

The Brigadier's Daughter	Catherine March
The Wicked Baron	Sarah Mallory
His Runaway Maiden	June Francis

MEDICAL™

Wanted: A Father for her Twins	Emily Forbes
Bride on the Children's Ward	Lucy Clark
The Rebel of Penhally Bay	Caroline Anderson
Marrying the Playboy Doctor	Laura Iding

™ MILLS & BOON®

AUGUST 2009 LARGE PRINT TITLES

ROMANCE

The Spanish Billionaire's Pregnant Wife	Lynne Graham
The Italian's Ruthless Marriage Command	Helen Bianchin
The Brunelli Baby Bargain	Kim Lawrence
The French Tycoon's Pregnant Mistress	Abby Green
Diamond in the Rough	Diana Palmer
Secret Baby, Surprise Parents	Liz Fielding
The Rebel King	Melissa James
Nine-to-Five Bride	Jennie Adams

HISTORICAL

The Disgraceful Mr Ravenhurst	Louise Allen
The Duke's Cinderella Bride	Carole Mortimer
Impoverished Miss, Convenient Wife	Michelle Styles

MEDICAL™

Children's Doctor, Society Bride	Joanna Neil
The Heart Surgeon's Baby Surprise	Meredith Webber
A Wife for the Baby Doctor	Josie Metcalfe
The Royal Doctor's Bride	Jessica Matthews
Outback Doctor, English Bride	Leah Martyn
Surgeon Boss, Surprise Dad	Janice Lynn

ROMANCE

A Bride for His Majesty's Pleasure	Penny Jordan
The Master Player	Emma Darcy
The Infamous Italian's Secret Baby	Carole Mortimer
The Millionaire's Christmas Wife	Helen Brooks
Duty, Desire and the Desert King	Jane Porter
Royal Love-Child, Forbidden Marriage	Kate Hewitt
One-Night Mistress...Convenient Wife	Anne McAllister
Prince of Montéz, Pregnant Mistress	Sabrina Philips
The Count of Castelfino	Christina Hollis
Beauty and the Billionaire	Barbara Dunlop
Crowned: The Palace Nanny	Marion Lennox
Christmas Angel for the Billionaire	Liz Fielding
Under the Boss's Mistletoe	Jessica Hart
Jingle-Bell Baby	Linda Goodnight
The Magic of a Family Christmas	Susan Meier
Mistletoe & Marriage	Patricia Thayer & Donna Alward
Her Baby Out of the Blue	Alison Roberts
A Doctor, A Nurse: A Christmas Baby	Amy Andrews

HISTORICAL

Devilish Lord, Mysterious Miss	Annie Burrows
To Kiss a Count	Amanda McCabe
The Earl and the Governess	Sarah Elliott

MEDICAL™

Country Midwife, Christmas Bride	Abigail Gordon
Greek Doctor: One Magical Christmas	Meredith Webber
Spanish Doctor, Pregnant Midwife	Anne Fraser
Expecting a Christmas Miracle	Laura Iding

0809 Gen Std LP

SEPTEMBER 2009 LARGE PRINT TITLES

ROMANCE

The Sicilian Boss's Mistress	Penny Jordan
Pregnant with the Billionaire's Baby	Carole Mortimer
The Venadicci Marriage Vengeance	Melanie Milburne
The Ruthless Billionaire's Virgin	Susan Stephens
Italian Tycoon, Secret Son	Lucy Gordon
Adopted: Family in a Million	Barbara McMahon
The Billionaire's Baby	Nicola Marsh
Blind-Date Baby	Fiona Harper

HISTORICAL

Lord Braybrook's Penniless Bride	Elizabeth Rolls
A Country Miss in Hanover Square	Anne Herries
Chosen for the Marriage Bed	Anne O'Brien

MEDICAL™

The Children's Doctor's Special Proposal	Kate Hardy
English Doctor, Italian Bride	Carol Marinelli
The Doctor's Baby Bombshell	Jennifer Taylor
Emergency: Single Dad, Mother Needed	Laura Iding
The Doctor Claims His Bride	Fiona Lowe
Assignment: Baby	Lynne Marshall

'Then why didn't you tell me the truth? Why did you let me think it didn't matter about me?'

'Because I was frightened you'd be upset.' Ann and Sasha both shifted and looked across to the sofa. 'Look, Eden, I knew you— I knew you would hate hurting them, his parents' feelings. But then they would have banned you from seeing Sasha, remembering, or if they could understand you as well. They're experts—' At or it means forgetting, what they were. And they weren't, were? I figured telling you it was my idea would at least give you reason to hate, like he did, you more.' She still was.

Eden shook her head in wonder. 'All those years I thought I'd done something wrong, but now you tell me that wasn't because—'

'You hadn't done anything wrong.'

'And you didn't think to fight his parents? To tell them you weren't being fair?' to Mollie, come?'

'Not then, then. I was ashamed, I couldn't even—I was so trying and it all meant that purpose.' 'Well, you couldn't be proud of all he—you, though—his parents' quarrels little to do with my upbringing?'

Eden smiled. 'You had a lot of nerve.'

'What is Sasha like?'

'Right.' She smiled and though she gave a moment, once, her Mollie'd come to—any more—'she laughed—would find left her hands, palm to Mr Gompie.' I couldn't let go of it—she lost her—

'Now—it's my turn to leave, if—'

She crossed, 'Well my?' Sasha' heart with. She walked down to the chair opposite where he sat and lowered herself into it.

'So tell me—what's been happening with your life during the past twelve years?'

'It's the sort of thing that's hard to understand—'